THE ENGINEER'S NEMESIS

A COZY FANTASY HISTORICAL MYSTERY

LADY GEORGIA BRUNEL MYSTERIES
BOOK THREE

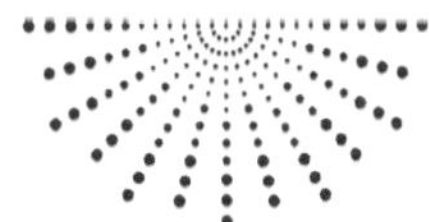

SHELLEY ADINA

Copyright © 2025 by Shelley Adina Senft Bates

All rights reserved. No part of this publication may be reproduced, distributed or transmitted in any form or by any means, including photocopying, recording, or other electronic or mechanical methods, without the prior written permission of the publisher, except in the case of brief quotations embodied in critical reviews and certain other noncommercial uses permitted by copyright law. For permission requests, write to the publisher at moonshellbooks.com.

This is a work of cozy fantasy and science fiction. Names, characters, places, and incidents are a product of the author's imagination. Locales and public names are sometimes used for atmospheric purposes. Any resemblance to actual people, living or dead, or to businesses, companies, events, institutions, or locales is completely coincidental.

Cover art by Jenny Zemanek. Images used under license.

The Engineer's Nemesis / Shelley Adina—1st ed.

ISBN 978-1-963929-45-4 R060325

❀ Formatted with Vellum

PRAISE FOR SHELLEY ADINA

"The plot is complex, the characters well considered, the story well crafted, full of twists and turns, not all of them expected. But the gentleness that marked the first novel is here again. It is a fun tale, with characters you want to spend time with. A tale of gentle lightness, it's just nice escapist fun, written to entertain and entertain it does. Genteel light, if you will, a genre all [Adina's] own, which has much to recommend it. I look forward to the next."

— THE PASSING PLACE, ON *THE AUTOMATON EMPRESS*

"I always love a well-written steampunk mystery that is clean, and *The Clockwork City* definitely fits all these criteria. The story is engaging, and the cast of characters play well together even if they aren't playing nice."

— BLOOMING WITH BOOKS, ON *THE CLOCKWORK CITY*

"Shelley Adina is quickly becoming a go-to author for fun, clean steampunk adventures! This delightful mystery completely pulled me in and had me quickly turning the pages. It's a fantastic introduction to a new series I'm looking forward to reading more of."

— MELISSA'S BOOKSHELF, ON THE CLOCKWORK CITY

THE ENGINEER'S NEMESIS

CHAPTER ONE

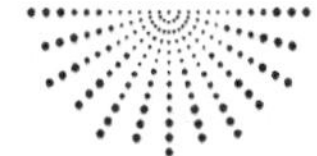

OVER PROVENCE

No, no, go not to Lethe, neither twist
Wolf's bane, tight-rooted, for its poisonous wine
Nor suffer thy pale forehead to be kissed
By nightshade, ruby grape of Proserpine...
—John Keats, Ode on Melancholy

Sunday, May 26, 1895

*L*ady Georgia Brunel stood at the helm of the airship *Helena*, the most modern and elegant civilian vessel of which the Zeppelin Airship Works was capable, and peered into the misty distance.

A sort of crenellation thrust up in the faraway haze. "That must be the Chateau de Valmy," she said, in a tone less certain than she had intended.

Her aunt by marriage, Millicent Brunel, whose forefinger lay upon the navigation chart as though holding it down in a high wind, nodded in agreement. "We have just passed over the confluence of the Rhône with the Rivière Valmy. In ten

"

miles we should see the river directed into the canal system that forms the lake. From the house, it is only half a mile to the sea."

A few minutes of gentle flight proved her correct, and Georgia's breathing eased. "I am glad that our first introduction to the vicomte will not be the result of a search party being called out for us. Goodness, I wonder when these concentric circles of canals were built? What a very ambitious project."

"I'm quite certain we will hear all about it," Millie said. "Didn't you say he was an engineer before he acceded to the title?"

"Yes. Anne thought she was marrying a man twenty years older than she, and established as a professor at the University of Edinburgh. She expected they would spend their lives together in Scotland. Neither of them knew, apparently, that he was the next heir. He knew some members of the French side of the family, of course, but the heirs preceding him seem to have had bad luck in reproducing."

"Life is full of odd surprises," Millie said absently. "*Helena*, circle the chateau and begin our descent. Georgia, the airfield seems to be only a short walk down a hedged avenue, and then over a bridge to the house. The lake might have been built for defense, but perhaps in these enlightened days, it is more for beauty … and irrigation."

Provence was a dry, rocky country, with outcroppings standing white in the sun, and rivers cutting through canyons as efficiently as the chisel of any Roman mason. However, if the vineyards and endless fields of lavender were any indication, it was nothing if not fertile. And the light! Georgia did not have much of a painter's soul, being much more inclined to figuring out the gleaming innards of *Helena*'s operation, and piloting a landau for the sheer joy of it, but even she could appreciate the light of the sinking sun into the glittering doorstep of the sea.

Perhaps, after all they had endured lately, she might have time for a painting or two in her sadly neglected sketchbook.

Helena sank to the ground with a graceful curtsey in a spacious field that had been planted, not with grass, but with some hardy herb that gave off a delicious scent as the ground crew reefed her down to the mooring irons. Two other well-maintained ships shared the field, both flying French colors.

At the bottom of the gangway, Millie breathed deeply. "Creeping thyme. How delightful. And this, I presume, is our hostess?"

Speeding down the graveled avenue came a contraption that defined the word *rattle-trap*. The front half might have once been an ancient landau, and the rear half seemed to have begun its life as a wagon. The engine puttered to a stop and the woman in the pilot's chair leaped out of it, flinging her arms wide. "Georgia!"

"Anne! My goodness, this is quite the reception—what on earth is that?" She was engulfed in a lavender-scented hug that squeezed the breath out of her. The former Anne McLeod was a tall, redheaded woman in the best Scottish tradition, more suited to moors and tweed than French lace and white voile. But her eyes sparkled and she appeared to be blooming with good health, so evidently life at the chateau suited her.

"That, my dear, is my husband's cart-of-all-work, ideal for putting luggage in. Come, you must introduce me to your dear aunt, of whom I have heard so much."

Georgia did so, whereupon Millie promptly disappeared

into Anne's hug of greeting. Once released, Millie adjusted her hat and beamed at such clear evidence of welcome. Goodness knew she had endured welcomes in her own family where the best that could be said of them was that they were not openly insulting. In short order, their valises and a hatbox or two were stowed in the rear of the cart.

"Is this all?" Anne said, hands on hips. "Please tell me you mean to stay for more than a single night."

"Indeed we do," Georgia said. "But we have just unpacked our traveling trunks into *Helena*'s closets, and were not certain of the situation here, so did not pack them up again."

"*Helena*." Anne's gaze met hers. "What a fine and appropriate name for a ship."

"I think my daughter would have approved." She blinked back the moisture in her eyes as she and Millie boarded the conveyance. "Now, I am anxious to meet your handsome vicomte. Let us begin our holiday with an introduction as soon as may be."

Georgia regretted her words immediately, as Anne wheeled the contraption about and they raced down the avenue at such a speed that she had to hold her hat on her hair with both hands. Had she been more familiar with Anne's skills as a pilot, she would have tied the lot down with a chiffon scarf. The Italian cypresses on either side flew by, until they were decanted onto a broad terrace dotted with huge stone urns bursting with bougainvillea, oleander, and poppies. A bridge led over the moat directly into the forecourt of the chateau, its paving gleaming with cleanliness and the gravel so white in the sun one risked crows' feet about the eyes from squinting.

"My hat is no match for this sun," Millie said breathlessly as she climbed out. "I shall have to find some wider brims."

"I have any number of them," Anne assured her. "Think of them as your own while you are here. Have you bathing costumes?"

Millie could only laugh in disbelief. Anne might as well have asked if they had rocket rucksacks.

"By that I deduce you do not. Never mind—I have several. I would suggest we dispense with them altogether, but since we have rather a party staying, that would hardly be proper, would it?" Her lips twitched into a wicked grin. "When we get rid of them, however ..."

"Anne!" Georgia protested, laughing. "How large is your party? I do hope we are not intruding."

"Not in the least. It's only some of the neighbors and a relative or two, here for my husband's birthday celebration this evening. He is fifty-nine, and vows this shall be the last."

Georgia nodded wisely. "I believe I said the same at twenty-nine. Sadly, the powers that be were not listening."

"Pish posh." Anne bumped her shoulder as they walked in through the double oak doors. "That English complexion of yours will never fail you. Don't you agree, Miss Brunel?"

"Entirely," Millie said. "And you must call me Millie. I feel as if I've known you forever. Georgia used to read me portions of your letters at Langford Park, and show me your paintings in the margins."

"Anne is a much better painter than I will ever be," Georgia said, surrendering her valise and hatbox to a strapping footman. "Ought we to change before we meet your guests?"

Anne took her shoulders in both hands and gazed at her with

mock sternness. "None of that nonsense here." She released her and indicated her own linen skirt, stark and plain except for the vivid leaf-green of its color, and the voile waist that showed her fine throat. "As I tell the children, at home we come to tea as we are, do what we like, and only speak to people who amuse us. We do, however, dress for dinner. One may commit any number of *faux pas* here and get away with it, but not that."

She couldn't possibly be serious. Smiling, Georgia took Millie's arm and followed her friend into a large drawing room, hung with pale blue silk draperies so fine they billowed in the breeze coming in through the open windows. Sofas were arranged in conversational groupings, upholstered in silver and blue striped fabric, no doubt chosen to draw the eye outdoors, where the gardens and canals gave onto a distant view of the sea.

Georgia dragged her gaze back inside, where Anne was leading over a tall gentleman with silver in his dark hair, who could only be the Vicomte de Valmy.

"*Mon cher*, may I present my dear friend Georgia Brunel, Lady Langford, and her aunt by marriage, Miss Millicent Brunel. Ladies, my husband, Gregory Campbell."

Georgia and Millie dipped into curtsies, and he took each of their hands and squeezed them, his azure-blue eyes sparkling with delight. "I cannot tell you how happy I am to welcome you to our home," he said. "I trust you had a good flight here from Bavaria?" He glanced over her shoulder. "One of the neighbors is a meteorological sort, often in Geneva at the international airfield. He was quite convinced that you might run into heavy weather over the Alps."

"No indeed," Millie said. "I plotted a course that took us

farther north and west, and then straight down the Rhône until we reached the Rivière Valmy."

"You plotted it?" His eyebrows rose. "What did your crew have to say to that?"

"I agreed with it completely," Georgia said with a smile, then at his obvious confusion, explained, "We have no crew. We pilot *Helena* ourselves. My aunt is a natural, as the Texicans say. It turns out she has an eye for land forms that did not steer us awry even once."

"Bless my soul," de Valmy said. "Villiers, did you hear that? These ladies have flown that lovely vessel all this way themselves."

They were swiftly introduced to Stefan Villiers, the meteorological chap. "This is most unexpected," he said, his English charmingly accented. "A century ago, it was common to see Frenchwomen enjoying powered flight—Madame Sophie Blanchard and her daughter Celeste being the most notable—but in this day and age one does not see it so often."

"In England and the Fifteen Colonies many women pilot their own ships," Millie said.

"Women of the mechanical and military kind, indeed yes. But gentlewomen?"

He made it sound as shocking as sea-bathing without benefit of costume. Georgia raised a brow. "A gentlewoman of independent means may go where she pleases, whether by train, steam landau, sailboat, or airship. All of which I pilot—less the train, of course."

"I am certain you could drive a train, too, my dear lady," de Valmy said with an admiring smile, when Villiers seemed too flummoxed to reply. "Heaven forbid I should deny *la vicomtesse* any means of getting where she wishes to go. For I know she will do it anyway, and leave me sneezing in the dust."

"You would not be so foolish," Anne said affectionately, slipping her arm into his. "Come, help me do the honors."

Georgia and Millie were introduced to Villiers' wife and son, who lived on an estate a mile or two off, and to two professors from Manchester who were related in some way to the vicomte that Georgia did not follow. They were in the south of France for a visit following a fossil-hunting trip in Normandy and Picardy.

"Such specimens we found!" Sibyl Campbell, a lady of uncertain age but as tanned as though she had been in the Mediterranean sun for weeks, clasped her hands. "All crated up and sent back to the university, but oh my—" She seemed unable to express her satisfaction.

"What my sister means is that we may have discovered proof of the existence of an entirely new genus of snail in the Cetaceous layer." Roger Campbell gazed at them in expectant delight, the way new parents might wait for congratulations.

"How wonderful!" Millie said. "How many kinds of snail have been discovered from that period?"

"We fossil hunters refer to geologic time in *epochs*, dear lady. As to number, there are, sadly, few. We are only beginning to understand the land forms that existed then, which would have made a suitable environment for the divergence of species, the knowledge of which would give us a place to look."

"We suspect there may be exciting finds of that kind along this coast as well, however," Sibyl added.

Georgia felt her eyelids closing of their own accord, and blinked herself back to attention as Anne said, "Do not give them an audience, Millie, or you will learn far more than you ever wanted to about coprolites."

"What are—"

"This way, my dears!"

Georgia smiled over her shoulder at the Campbells, who did not seem offended in the least, but launched into a lively discussion comprehensible only to themselves.

"What on earth is a coprolite?" Millie persisted. "Animal, vegetable, or mineral?"

Anne snickered, just the way she used to at St. Cecelia's Academy for Young Ladies when making fun of the teachers. "They are, er, the fossilized excrement of a once living creature."

After a moment, Millie said, "Remind me never to be trapped alone in conversation with either of the Campbells, then, would you, Georgia?"

"You may depend upon it."

Along with the fossil hunters, the visiting guests included Manon Fleury, a cousin a year or two younger than Georgia, who was stopping at the chateau before meeting her husband and family in Nantes and boarding a transatlantic airship for New York.

"I thought *Persephone* departed from Paris," Georgia said. "Has the Astor line expanded?"

"*Non, madame,*" Manon said. "These are van Meere ships. They may be smaller than *Persephone*, but only slightly, and are very modern and fast."

"Any connection to Mr Cornelius van Meere?" she asked, since Millie refused to.

"Yes, he is the owner of the line." Manon twinkled at some private thought. "He is a very talented engineer, they say. And a single man. There is many a lady who books passage on his ships hoping to meet the owner by chance on the voyage."

"Is that so?" Millie was finally goaded into saying.

"Oh yes. Myself, I am happily married, but *ma mere*, who travels with us next week … well, let us just say that she is an optimist, and most observant."

Millie was silenced once more—or was possibly exerting the utmost in self-control. Georgia smiled at Madame Fleury and said, "Then I hope she has good hunting. Do excuse us. I am hoping to persuade Anne to take us up to meet the children."

"Ah, *les petites* Elodie and Elise. They are charming—about the same age as my own Robert." Her smile seemed to set. "And now that our dear Anne is *enceinte* once again, perhaps the twins will have a brother in the autumn, too."

Georgia turned to Anne in astonishment. "Are you really? Oh, I am so pleased." She hugged her with one arm about the waist as Anne directed them to the wide oak staircase in the main hall.

"I meant to tell you later, but in fact, Manon told *me* when she arrived, the clever minx. She studied to become a doctor, you know, but once she met Edouard, her university career was all over, and she rapidly became the mother of four. Such a surprise this was to both Gregory and me. Imagine, the mother of twins and I missed the signs altogether. He, of course, is over the moon."

Georgia well remembered experiencing the signs, counting them up like gold, turning them over and over like precious coins. And then… She shook away the memories, which had no place in this bright house full of conversation and affection.

Elodie and Elise were on the third floor with their governess, laboring over sums in a suite of rooms that extended half the length of the chateau. They looked to be about eight, and had inherited their father's dark hair and azure eyes. Released from their studies, they ran downstairs to find their tea, and Anne took Georgia and Millie back down to the second-floor gallery to their rooms.

"My goodness, how lovely." Georgia's valise and hatbox were already in a south-facing room with a view of the ocean. Millie's room lay across the hall, overlooking the lake and a knot garden of at least an acre, made entirely of dozens of varieties of roses.

"Oh, Anne," she sighed. "Did Georgia tell you that gardens are my delight? How very kind of you to allow me to sit in this window seat and gaze at this one for as many hours as I please."

"Oh, I hope you will not be up here all the time," Anne said. "No, my friend did not say a word, but I am happy you like the room. We shall be sure to spend lots of time in the garden. I drive Monsieur Laurent a wee bit mad, always floating about nipping the buds off things and spoiling his compositions with my trowels and seedlings."

"He is your gardener?" Georgia asked.

"He is more than a gardener. He is in great demand along the Loire—all those sixteenth-century chateaux, you know— and the families can't simply plant any old thing. They must have their gardens *designed* if they do not like the ancient plantings."

"Of course they do," said Millie with a roll of the eyes.

"His wife is our chef, and woe betide you if you set foot in her herb garden, which is at least an acre also. I made the mistake of attempting to plant just the tiniest, most innocuous little lavender variety out there once, since she didn't have any and I love it. And oh, my goodness, she practically chased me inside with the cleaver she happened to have in her hand."

"Gracious," Georgia said faintly. "I'd have sacked her."

"One doesn't sack the finest cook in Provence," Anne said flatly. "And she did apologize. But I learned my lesson. And you must, too. I do not want you losing body parts because you want a bit of lemon for your tea."

"Duly noted," Millie said. "I think there are gardens enough on the estate that we will not need to invade Madame Laurent's domain."

"I smell lavender in the house," Georgia said. "You must have planted your little specimen somewhere."

"We are surrounded by it. One of our tenants has at least ten acres. For the parfumiers, you know. But he brings me great bunches of it for the house … and planted a lovely border of it just below the terrace. That is likely what you smell. Speaking of tea, you must be parched," Anne said. "I have had mine earlier, but I will set the example and eat everything in sight. One thing about expecting a little blessing —I can eat for two and Gregory cannot tell me I mustn't."

CHAPTER TWO

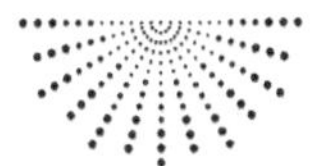

$\mathcal{T}$ea was delightful, but Georgia observed that Millie was tiring of the constant chatter in two languages, despite her facility with both. When she suggested a walk in the gardens, Anne instantly agreed it would be the very thing.

"You'll find straw hats of every description on both sides of the west door here on the ground floor," she said, leading them across the grand entry hall. "My office and my husband's are both down the same corridor, as well as those of the estate manager and Monsieur and Madame Chouinard, our butler and housekeeper. It is the tradition, you know, to rest in the afternoon during the heat of the day. Gregory certainly enjoys the habit, and I shall fall asleep standing, like a horse, if I do not find my bed soon."

Thus released, Georgia and Millie wasted no time in finding suitable straw hats in Anne's collection and stepping out of doors.

"Bliss," Millie sighed. "I must say, I have no trouble with the heat of the afternoon. While the company is very pleasant, and your friend Anne a breath of fresh air, I find I need a rest more of the mind than of the body."

"As do I." Georgia followed a graveled path in a direction she hoped would take them to the knot garden of roses. "What do you think of our fellow guests?"

"I do not know enough of them to form an opinion," Millie said. "Isn't it singular that the only heir in the de Valmy family was an obscure engineer in Scotland? How did that come about, I wonder?"

"Do you have the courage to ask him?" Georgia teased.

"Perhaps not. It is none of my business."

"All I know is what Anne has told me in her letters. His lordship's branch of the family came to Scotland two centuries ago in the train of Mary, Queen of Scots, and inter-married in the Campbell clan. He and Anne had been married ten years and were still in Edinburgh when the news came that some great-uncle or other had passed away in France. It turned out he had been the vicomte, and the father of four girls and a young son."

"Oh dear," Millie said wryly. "And of course a capable young woman could not manage this place, could she?"

"Honestly, primogeniture might have been useful in the thirteenth century, when a strong sword arm was necessary, but now it is merely inconvenient," Georgia said by way of agreement. "I am not clear how they finally got round to Gregory Campbell, but it took the deaths of the boy and a much older second cousin before a French lawyer arrived in Edinburgh to announce that he was the latest heir to the place."

"Thereby upending their lives?"

"His, certainly. He was about to join forces with a friend of his, a professor of engineering called Linden, and establish a business on two continents." Georgia thought for a moment. "Something to do with trains. In any case, the friend and his wife went to the Texican Territories for the trains, and were never seen again. And Gregory became the fourteenth Vicomte de Valmy."

"Goodness. I am sorry about the Lindens. As for the Campbells, we must believe that it was for the best, Georgia," Millie said. "They do seem happy."

"They do," she agreed. "Look, here is the garden."

"Doesn't it smell divine? Did you ever see so many varieties of rose in your life?" Ecstatic, Millie bent to sniff a massive golden bloom the size of a dessert plate. "I do wish each one had a plaque at the base, as they did in the Medicinal Gardens in Munich. So well organized. One does not have to ask about each flower and risk annoying one's companions."

Georgia and Millie wandered happily about, sniffing and exclaiming over colors, before discovering a gate in the hedge that gave on to a vast meadow filled with red and gold poppies and dozens of varieties of wildflowers. She was just about to get Millie's attention and suggest a walk to the sea, when the window along from Millie's room opened and a figure leaned out.

"Are you enjoying yourselves?" Manon Fleury called down. "What enormous hats you have found."

"Very much," Millie called back. "Will you join us?"

"Not I. The sun and I have an agreement. He is very fierce, and I stay indoors until his temper softens."

Georgia waved, and Manon closed the window and withdrew. Then they sallied forth through the gate and found a path that had been mowed through the wildflowers, meandering down the slope under the shade of widely scattered cedars, bent no doubt by the wind off the sea.

"A pity so many flowers had to be cut down," Millie said.

"But it is so much easier to walk together without risking stains and insects. Millie, did you happen to notice Manon earlier, when we were talking about Anne's little blessing arriving in the autumn?"

"She did not seem as pleased at the prospect as one might have expected. But the impression was gone before I could really be sure I had seen it."

"Hm."

"Georgia."

"Yes?" She bent to pick a stalk of Queen Anne's Lace. "This reminds me of the lace on Anne's blouse."

"Do not change the subject. We must not imagine trouble where none exists."

"Of course not. She may have had a stomach cramp. Or eaten too many petits fours. Manon Fleury seems like a perfectly agreeable person. Certainly not the sort to begrudge a woman an heir to what seems to be a prosperous estate." Georgia picked a spray of blue bachelor buttons, and several poppies, and wondered if she might scandalize the guests if she put them in her hair.

"My thoughts exactly. Her little Robert cannot inherit in any case, can he? The line cannot pass through the mother."

"We do not know how French law operates. And it is none of our business in any case." Georgia had to laugh at herself. "How disappointed Teddy would be to hear us. He would say our brushes with evil have left a stain. And that, I must admit, distresses me."

"Surely he would not wish you to be careless of the troubles of others?"

"Certainly not. But he would not like to hear us borrowing trouble, either. We must curb the tendency, and develop a sunnier outlook. Here. Wait a moment." She tucked all her flowers in Millie's hatband. "Now you look like a meadow nymph. How I wish Mr van Meere could see you."

Millie snorted, and marched away down the path at such a pace that Georgia had to skip to keep up. The sandstone cliffs sloped down to the azure sea to form a beautiful crescent beach below, perfect for sea-bathing.

"I am going to hold Anne to her promise," Georgia said, fanning herself with her hat. "A dip in that sea would be divine."

"With or without benefit of bathing costume?"

"Either way," Georgia said pertly. "As long as there are no observers. Look—is that the Campbells?"

"I do not see as well as you, but I think so." Millie took her arm. "Come, let us go back. I do not wish to be drawn from my happy contemplation of wildflowers into conversation about ... coprolites. Or anything else of a geologic nature."

"Even if it were a fossil of a fern?"

"Even then. I prefer the living to the very long dead."

Georgia had to agree. They wound their way back to the knot garden, and from there it was only a short distance to the avenue and *Helena*.

"I wonder if there might be something in the communications cage," Millie said far too innocently.

"You go look. Shall we change for dinner here, or take our dresses down, do you think?"

"Change here," Millie called as she made her way astern.

She returned in a minute or two bearing a letter, and Georgia's pulse jumped. If her own body had not told her from whom that buff envelope had come, the glow in Millie's face would have.

Georgia forced herself to sit quietly on the sofa in the saloon while Millie opened the letter. Her efforts at patience were rewarded when Millie handed over a cleverly folded sheet with *Lady Langford* written on it in a spiky, cramped hand. The folding had to be Marcus's work. She knew the trick of it, however, since she had taught him and Cora how to fold paper as securely as any lock.

My lady,

I hope this finds the two of you well. We're fine, though Marcus is moping. He won't admit it, but he misses Cora. I can understand his feelings, though I'm perfectly willing to admit that I do miss you.

We've had a change in plan since we set our course for home. A letter came from one Sir Andrew Malvern, who is on the organizing committee for this colloquium shindig in September. Seems they've finally settled on a place to have it. I suppose Blenheim wasn't available. A friend of his has unexpectedly inherited an earldom that includes a house big enough for the windbags to blow at length, and a private airfield that will accommodate even Foresight. Since she's as big as an island, this suits us. Their invitation to Cornelius to join the committee met with a blunt refusal, but he agreed to meet at this house to talk over the guest list and the logistics of the various installations.

Do you know these folks? The Earl and Countess of Falmouth.

Charts are no help for such things as estates, but the Seacombe family pile isn't far along the coast. Not that I plan to stop by for a visit in this century.

September can't come fast enough. Don't know if there will be time to fly to the ranch and back with all this chin-wagging—but at least Marcus will get some schooling while he's here. I've engaged a tutor to fly with us for the time being, much to his disgust. And I admit I like the thought of being within a day's flight of you, for as long as that lasts. I hope you're enjoying the sunshine and the company of your friend. You deserve every good and lovely thing.

My regards to Miss Brunel. Cornelius has written her a screed. He is even worse off than me. I'm not sure either of us will make it to June without seeing you both, never mind September.

Your own

Dustin

June was only six days away. Was Dustin Seacombe being metaphorical, or was there really a chance that *Foresight* might loom out of the clouds like a great thunderhead, and land in the wildflower meadow? Anticipation bubbled up inside her like an eternally hopeful spring.

When Millie looked up from her letter, she was actually blushing. Georgia pretended not to notice, but only because her own cheeks were feeling rather warm.

"They have not gone," Millie said, her eyes sparkling. "Such a pair they are, forever leaving and always coming back."

"You can't blame them for last time," Georgia pointed out. "No one can predict air pirates."

"True." Millie looked down as though searching for a particular line. A small smile told Georgia she had found it. "I am not complaining, mind you. But Cornelius may simply become so impatient with all this backing and forthing that he will purchase an estate in England and be done with it."

It was on the tip of Georgia's tongue to say, *And you will be its mistress.* But she did not. "Time will tell. Shall we dress and walk down to the house?"

Millie folded up her letter and located her reticule to tuck it inside. "I suppose we must. They will be gathering on the terrace for drinks soon. We were promised lavender lemonade. I have been looking forward to it very much. Do you suppose we might enjoy some this evening?"

"I think it would be difficult to avoid it. I envision Madame Laurent despairing of innovative ways to use lavender when yet another basket arrives from their tenant."

They put on the lightest of their evening dresses and decided together that no one would notice if they were supported by only two petticoats, not three. And no tiara. This was pushing informality to quite a degree, Georgia had to admit. "If I am sent to my room to change, I shall stamp my foot and refuse," she said as they walked down the gravel avenue toward the bridge.

As it turned out, only Anne, with the reputation of the title to consider, had come down in full evening dress. The other women had exchanged white voile and ruffles for light silk and lace, and Manon wore a delightful lace cap and fichu that was clearly part of the festive costume for women in the region. No one wore a tiara. Such a relief—they became so heavy after an hour or two.

Conversation out on the terrace ranged from sailboat racing to irrigation to the latest headlines in the newspapers. Millie was delighted to be offered a tall glass of lavender lemonade, while Georgia accepted a glass of wine so rich and golden it was like liquid sunshine.

"From our own vineyard," the vicomte told her. Though something seemed to be bothering him. His breathing seemed the result of conscious effort, not ease. Perhaps it was the many acres of blooming flowers, which she had heard could affect one's nose and eyes. "The soil here looks appalling to the uneducated eye, but the *terroir* produces unparalleled Viognier grapes."

"It is lovely," she said, though she had never heard of a Viognier grape. "Like everything I have seen here. It is a wonder your guests can ever bring themselves to leave."

He gave a small smile. "I hope you will stay for as long as you like. Anne tells me you have been traveling, and having adventures in the best—best Isabella Bird tradition." He pressed his forearm to his stomach, clearly intending to disguise some upset.

Was his face a little pale? But it would not do to ask intrusive questions in front of his guests. Perhaps it was the result of being out on a warm day. "It is a compliment to join such company, even in the imagination," she said. "But I must confess I am happiest in my own nest, with my son sprawled in front of the fire and Millie curled up on the sofa, reading aloud the latest from Sir Arthur Conan Doyle."

"I feel the same." He gazed out across the orderly lawns, past the wildflower fields, to the sea in the distance. "I once thought that Scotland was the most beautiful place a man could live. Raw, wild, and a challenge to the strong. But all our children have been b-born here, and I have gained an appreciation for deep roots and enduring b-beauty."

"And excellent wine," Georgia added, lifting her glass and hoping her smile disguised her concern.

"I am glad you are here to share it—as well as the last birthday I will ever admit to."

In the depths of the house, a bell rang.

"That is certainly worth celebrating." She accepted his arm and allowed him to escort her in to dinner. Under her hand, she could feel him trembling.

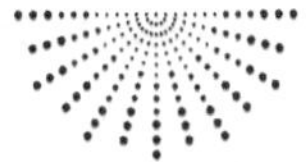

illie had rather agreed with Georgia on the subject of sacking someone who would brandish a cleaver at the mistress of the house, but the first bite of the delicious sole in lemon sauce convinced her that Anne Campbell had done the right thing in keeping Madame Laurent on. The sole … the duck … the salads fresh from the garden … the soufflé light as air and tasting of cucumber … well, one simply didn't get food like this in England, did one?

Not that she would ever allow her stomach to overrule her intellect, but allowances certainly ought to be made.

By the time a tarte tatin and hazelnut and *crème fraîche* meringues were brought in, night had fallen and the candles lit in the dining room. There were electricks, of course, running along the wainscoting and under the cornices, but there was nothing like the romance of candles on a lovely warm evening where the conversation was pleasant and each meringue a piece of art.

Millie sat between Monsieur Villiers and Anne Campbell at one end, while Georgia, who ranked second to *la vicomtesse,* sat at the vicomte's right hand. A tiny pleat had formed between her brows, but it was more than likely the geologist's conversation on her other side was the cause. As the meal progressed, Millie came to realize that the pleat was on his lordship's behalf. The vicomte seemed less enthusiastic about his dinner with each course. And he had been so gallant and smiling on the terrace, chatting with each of his guests and even attempting a chuckle at the witticisms of the geologist and his sister.

The sight of the tarte tatin made him look positively ill.

Millie stole a glance at Anne, to see her gaze fixed on her husband as though waiting for one more clench of his eyebrows before flying to his side. "Excuse me," she said to no one in particular, and laid down her napkin before doing exactly that. "My dear, are you ill?"

He looked up at her as though he wasn't certain who she was. "Yes," he said after a moment to consider the question. "I cannot feel my mouth."

She glanced over at his cousin, who had just crunched into an enormous bite of macaroon. "Roger, would you help me see his lordship to his room?"

The man actually stuffed the remainder of the macaroon into his mouth before rising and wiping the crumbs from his lips. "Certainly. Happy to oblige."

The conversation sagged to a stop as the vicomte left the dining room between the two of them, their arms supporting his back as though without help, he might crumple to the floor.

Manon Fleury put down her own napkin and rose. "Perhaps I may be of assistance." Millie thought this a touch presumptuous, until she remembered that the woman had had medical training.

With their party down by four, the guests seemed at a loss for what to do. But Georgia, the hostess of many a disastrous dinner party, rose to the occasion. "If everyone has finished their most excellent dinner, perhaps we might have coffee in the drawing room?" She glanced at the footman standing silently between two enormous cabinets filled with objets d'art, whereupon he bowed and vanished through the baize door.

In the drawing room, both Millie and Georgia did their best to make conversation, but the atmosphere was tense. When Manon Fleury came down, it was not to tell them that the attack had passed and *le vicomte* was feeling better, as Millie had hoped, but to lean over Stefan Villiers' chair and say quietly, "Is your man available to go for the physician?"

He rose immediately. "If he is not, I shall."

With a bow to the room in general, he hurried out.

"What is the matter with poor Gregory?" Sibyl Campbell demanded of her brother when he appeared in the doorway, looking worried. Manon passed him and went back upstairs without another word.

"Some stomach upset," he said. "Not fit to talk about in company, old girl."

"But he was perfectly well earlier, when we were having drinks. What could have upset him?"

"I expect the doctor will be able to tell us," Georgia said in a tone that clearly said, *May we please not speculate about our host?*

But Sibyl seemed to be one of those people who understood words to have only one meaning, that did not change with one's tone. "I thought the duck was underdone," she said. "Perhaps that was the culprit."

"The duck was perfectly cooked," Madame Villiers said stiffly. "In France, we do not cook our meat to the consistency of sand."

Sibyl retreated into the silence of high dudgeon, much to Millie's relief.

"Shall we have another sunny day tomorrow, do you think?" Georgia asked. When Madame Villiers replied in the affirmative, the conversation returned to boating, which apparently was the primary pursuit of the landowners along this balmy stretch of coast. The extent of Millie's experience with boats was Teddy's taking her punting on the Cherwell during a spring visit. The likelihood of either herself or Georgia going sailing was next to nothing … and if their host did not recover quickly, it was equally unlikely they would burden poor Anne by staying any longer. Nothing could be more awful than having a houseful of guests when one's beloved husband was ill and one wished to be at his bedside, not making sure geologists were fed and relatives seen off to catch their trains.

An hour of conversational fits and starts ensued before Monsieur Villiers returned with the doctor, who was met in the hall by Madame Fleury and hurried upstairs. Millie half hoped for some news of *le vicomte*'s condition, but all they received was a *"Bonne nuit,"* and a bow as the Villiers departed for their own home.

Together on one blue-and-silver striped sofa, Millie and Georgia regarded Sibyl and Roger on the other, across the empty coffee cups on the low carved table between them.

"Well," Roger said. "I suppose that's that. I was hoping for cards, but there seems nothing left to do but go to bed."

"It must be serious, don't you think?" Sibyl asked anxiously. "Why else would Anne stay above stairs and neglect her company?"

"I do not feel neglected," Millie said, her spine straight and her smile warm. "But I do agree. We all ate the same dishes, and are feeling no ill effects at all, so it cannot be something like undercooked duck. Does his lordship suffer from poor health in general?"

"No indeed. He was showing us a fossil bed and galloping up and down those rocks as easily as any goat only yesterday," Roger replied. "I do hope it's nothing catching. I cannot afford to be sick, with the symposium only a few weeks away."

"I am sure it isn't," Georgia said.

Millie had to admire her self-control in the face of such selfishness. Or perhaps it was merely single-mindedness, which often amounted to the same.

"I feel the most considerate thing we can do for our hosts is to conclude the evening and stay out of the way. Perhaps *le vicomte* will be well enough to open his birthday gifts at breakfast." She rose, and even Roger was gentleman enough not to remain seated. "Good night—sleep well."

Millie and Georgia climbed the stairs, with only the briefest pause on the landing as they heard the doors of the two cousins' rooms close. Georgia appeared to make up her mind. "I want to tap on Gregory's door and ask after him," she said. "Though I suspect that if Anne had news for us, she would have come and told us."

Millie had to agree. "I'm sure he will be recovered in the

morning. Stomach upsets often resolve themselves with a basin close at hand and a good rest."

But somehow her own room had little appeal, even with the scent of roses on the air. She hoped Georgia would not mind a bit of conversation in the delightful sitting area to one side of her bed, in front of the windows. She closed the door and advanced a little into the room, whereupon Georgia took off her shoes and sank onto the sofa, waving Millie to the other corner.

"I confess I am worried. The poor man looked awful. Did you hear him say he could not feel his mouth?"

"I was at the other end of the table. That is an odd remark to make. Did his eyes look normal?"

"The room was rather romantically lit," Georgia pointed out. "I noticed nothing unusual about his eyes, but his color was awful. I do hope the doctor can help him." After a moment, she said, "What do you think of the birthday guests now?"

Millie pursed her lips. "I think that regardless of *le vicomte*'s health, the sooner the geologists depart for their symposium, the better. Goodness me—compared to Mr Campbell, your erstwhile suitor the Archduke was a model of gentlemanly behavior."

Since they were alone, Georgia allowed herself a chuckle. "Isn't he appalling? Sibyl seems nice enough, though she tends to be overshadowed by the boorishness of her brother."

"The Villiers seem both kind and civil," Millie mused. "I had the impression that while the estates march together, the size of them makes it easier to visit in an airship rather than a landau."

"It is the same in England, depending on whether one is a

Blood or a Wit. But fancy the expense of a crew on hand at the airfield all the time. They certainly do not fly their own, if his surprise at our doing so was any indication."

Millie had to acknowledge the truth of that. "I did warm up to Manon Fleury in the end. She dotes on the little girls, doesn't she? I heard her say she has only one girl, and the other three are energetic boys."

Georgia covered a yawn with one hand. "It is rather early, but we have come a long way today."

Millie rose instantly. "Good night, then, dearest."

Georgia hugged her. "Sleep well, and we will hope for better news in the morning."

Monday, May 27 at 2:15 a.m.

Millie woke with a start to see a shadowy form bending over her, but her next breath told her at once who it was. Georgia kept sachets among her nightclothes scented with vanilla.

"What is it, dear?" she whispered.

"A sound woke me," Georgia whispered back. "A cry. From the family rooms."

"Then we must see if someone needs help."

Barefoot and wrapped in dressing gowns, they hurried down the gallery. A light shone from under the door of the *vicomte* and *vicomtesse*'s suite, whose rooms took up one whole side of the corridor that branched off from the gallery. Georgia knocked lightly, and when no reply was forthcoming, cautiously opened the door and peeked in.

"Anne?" she said softly. "Are you awake?"

With a glance of concern over her shoulder she slipped

inside, Millie just behind. There could be no danger of interrupting any private activity—every lamp was lit and every door standing open. From *le vicomte*'s room came a sound that reminded Millie of an animal in pain. The kind that often resulted in death.

They found Anne lying on top of the white duvet, one arm flung over her husband and her head upon his chest. She was sobbing as though her heart had just broken.

Georgia started forward, but Millie grabbed her wrist just in time. She had seen what Georgia clearly had not. "Georgia. He is gone. It is not our place."

Her voice was barely audible, but Anne lifted her head and stared at them. Her eyes were wild, her cheeks streaked with tears, her hair rumpled and falling out of its pins. Her evening dress lay tossed over a chair, and she seemed to have changed into a blouse and the green skirt she had worn earlier.

Despite the warmth of the house and the softness of the night air through the open windows, she was shivering.

"She is in shock," Georgia said. "Millie, run downstairs to the drawing room. I saw a bottle of brandy on a trolley between the windows. I shall find her a wrap."

When Millie returned with three snifters dangling from her fingers and the bottle in the other hand, Georgia was sitting on the bed, cradling Anne in her arms while she sobbed.

"I don't understand," Anne wailed while Millie swiftly poured and handed the brandy to Georgia. "He was perfectly w-well. And then he was not. And now he's d-dead!"

"I do not understand it either, dearest. Please take some of this. It will help, I promise."

Like a child, Anne took the glass in both hands and swallowed some of the brandy. She gasped, coughed, and then downed another gulp. Georgia handed Millie the snifter and Anne a handkerchief and she blew her nose and mopped her eyes. She was no less upset, but her color was better and she was not shaking quite so violently. The green cardigan Georgia had found looked well loved and cozy.

Georgia finished her own drink. Millie sipped hers rather more cautiously, but even so, the fumes were very strong.

"Thank you," Anne rasped. "Oh, Georgia, I don't know what to do. Am I to leave him lying here?"

Millie could not help but remember that dreadful morning when the horse had been discovered on the lawn at Langford Park, its rider's foot still in the stirrup. Millie had felt nothing but relief, Georgia only gratitude at a fate that had seen fit to free her from a violent man. And while this was a death as unexpected as it was mourned, the proprieties had to be observed.

"He is best here until the doctor returns," she murmured to Anne. "When did he say he would come?"

"I—he—" She took a deep breath. "At dawn. He said that often there was a change at dawn."

"What did he suspect was wrong?"

Anne's face crumpled with pain and derision, and Millie fetched another handkerchief from the chest of drawers. "Indigestion. Which is ridiculous—Gregory could eat bannock and haggis without so much as a twinge. And what was there about sole and duck that could cause such a thing? We eat them both at least twice a month. In any case, he threw them up just after midnight."

"Sometimes a heart attack comes disguised as indigestion," Millie ventured, passing the handkerchief.

Anne stared sightlessly past her, as though reliving the scene. "His heart was galloping as though he had run in from the cliffs instead of walking. But he was in bed. And then it slowed, and I thought he might improve. A moment later he clutched his chest and cried out my name. Oh, I felt so helpless! I ran to fetch Manon but she was not in her room. By the time I reached his side again, his poor heart had got over whatever fright it had and was beating at a normal speed. Then it slowed once more. And—" She choked. Swallowed. Looked from one to the other as tears overflowed down her cheeks. "And then it simply … stopped."

"That must have been when I heard you cry out," Georgia said. "I looked at the clock and it was two fifteen."

"What difference does the time make when my dearest love is dead?"

"None at all." She wiped her friend's face as tenderly as she had once comforted Teddy over some hurt administered by his father. "Would you like to stay with him a little longer while Millie and I do what must be done?"

"Y-yes." And then, "How am I going to tell the girls? Oh Georgia, how can I tell them the father they kissed good night is gone by morning?"

"You will bring them in and let them say farewell," Millie said quietly. When Georgia looked up in surprise, the words seemed to pour out of her. "I know it sounds as though it will give them pain—and it may—but I have never forgotten not being allowed to say good-bye to my mother. I was not permitted to see her at all, because we lived in India and burials occur very soon after death because of the heat. Instead, I hovered in the jasmine arbor, hoping my father would change his mind … because of course children could not attend a funeral in those days. So it was as though she simply left one day without even looking back for me." Millie felt the familiar ache under her breastbone, made of equal parts love and sorrow. She had never been able to bear the scent of jasmine since. "I believe I carry that wound even yet."

Anne's gaze had not left her face, and in her eyes was a dawning decision. "You are quite right. At daybreak, they may say good-bye, and we will mourn together."

"Millie and I will leave you now, dear. I will inform the butler and ask him to send for the doctor, and then to make arrangements with the priest. We will do all we can to help you through the next few days. They will be dreadful, but we will walk through the valley of the shadow together."

"Thank you." Anne turned Georgia's hand over and kissed the palm, then reached for Millie's and gave it a squeeze. "I am so glad you are here. I could not bear to face this with Roger and Sibyl my only comforts."

In spite of herself, a snort of unladylike laughter escaped Millie's self-control, and in the next moment, the three of them had slid to the Aubusson carpet. "Laughing like ducks. Again," Anne gasped. "Oh, how Gregory would have enjoyed seeing us."

"Perhaps he is laughing with us even now," Millie said, doing her best to get herself under control.

"He does—did appreciate a good laugh, even at his own expense." Anne's color was coming back, and a little life had returned to the grey eyes that had been swimming in tears. "Promise me I will laugh again."

"You will, and the girls with you," Georgia assured her.

They helped each other up and she and Millie left Anne to say her own farewells and keep watch through the night.

"Should not one of us stay with her?" Millie asked, pausing at the door of her own room.

"Would you have wanted someone hovering over you when your mother died?"

"No," Millie said, surprising herself. "I would have wanted her to myself if that was to be the last time."

Georgia nodded. "Then we will see that Anne receives that gift. I cannot sleep now. I shall dress and begin this awful business."

"I will, too. We had best divide and conquer."

CHAPTER FOUR

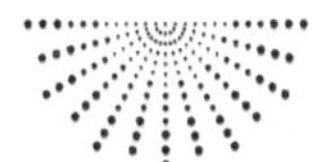

Georgia felt a little sorry for the doctor when he arrived, as it seemed he had been called away from the bed of a young mother in the town who had suffered a difficult birth. Now she was obliged to add to his burdens with the news that his friend *le vicomte* was dead.

"How can this be possible?" he murmured as Georgia met him in the entrance hall and showed him upstairs. "I would have testified at an inquest that it was only indigestion."

"Anne reports that his heartbeat was uneven after you had gone. Racing, then slowing, until at last it ceased altogether. I understand that a heart attack may sometimes present itself as indigestion."

"Of course I know that." He glared at her. "There is no need to educate me, young lady, on my own profession."

She took the long night into account before her temper got the best of her. "I do beg your pardon."

He breathed deeply. "Forgive me. It has been a difficult night. The third in a row. Who did you say you were?"

"I am Georgia Brunel, mother to the fifth Baron Langford,

of Langford Park in England," she said gently. "May I fetch you some refreshment before you go in?"

"*Non*, it would only delay the inevitable. So I have insulted a lady of quality, have I, to add to all my other shortcomings this evening?"

She took pity on the poor man and laid a comforting hand on his arm. "Doctor Besson, it was my fault for being presumptuous. Had *le vicomte* a history of heart trouble?"

"That is just it. He had not. In fact, for a man of his age he was in excellent health. Has *la vicomtesse* been with him all this time?"

"Yes. She wished it."

"Then perhaps you might encourage her to come away and get some rest. Are you a relative? There was a medical person among the guests—was it you?"

"No, I am merely an old school friend, here for *le vicomte*'s birthday. You must mean Madame Fleury. She has training but apparently chose marriage and children over a career in medicine. You saw her last evening—slender, dark hair, lovely eyes."

"Ah. I remember now. An efficient nurse, at any rate. Come along. We cannot put this off, much as I would like to."

Anne, worn out with weeping, allowed Georgia to lead her away to her own room, which was connected to that of her husband by a pair of dressing-rooms and a water closet the size of both of the latter put together.

"We never slept apart," Anne said sadly as Georgia turned down the sheets. "This is a lovely room, but I haven't spent much time in it in the ten years we've lived here."

"You need some rest," Georgia told her, patting the smooth cotton sheets. "And the doctor needs time for his examination. When the sun comes up, I will hold off the household until you and the girls have had time to say your goodbyes, and then I expect the rituals of the church will swing into action and the hour of privacy will be over."

"You are right." Anne slipped under the coverlet and let Georgia tuck her in. "I shall never sleep."

"Try to think of happy times. Of falling asleep in his arms. Of singing lullabies to the girls. I remember what a lovely voice you had at school."

"Gregory liked to hear me sing. His Scottish lark, he called me."

Georgia was tempted to assure her that there would be reasons to sing again, in time, but refrained. It seemed insulting to Gregory to encourage his wife not to mourn him.

"What was that song we had to learn in school?" Anne's voice was fading. "Something about larks."

Georgia took a moment to recall the tune. She was no lark, and in her brief career with the choir had been relegated to background noise. But she could do this for her friend.

"Have you seen her all of a morning
All of a morning, all of a morning."

It was a round, and Anne began it on the third line, humming.

"Have you heard the lark in the meadows
Singing to heaven, singing to heaven.
Let her lift your heart and hands then
Heart and hands then, heart and hands then,
Let her lift your hands into service

Your soul up to heaven
All of a morning.
Amen."

Georgia held the final notes until Anne's voice joined her at the end.

"That was it," Anne said softly. "They had to get in a reminder of the English work ethic, didn't they? Despite that, I always liked the thought of a soul being lifted up by a bird's music." Her eyes fluttered closed and, as she remembered she wasn't alone, opened again.

"As Gregory was lifted up by your singing," Georgia whispered. "Sleep now. I'll wake you when it's time."

She slipped out silently on bare feet, glancing back to see Anne's lashes lying at last upon her cheeks. The tune of the round that they had sung in assembly at St Cecelia's, on Sundays before church, played in her memory as she padded downstairs. It was just past four o'clock, and daylight would be upon them long before they were ready to face it.

She found Millie in serious conference with Monsieur Chouinard the butler and Madame Laurent in the office of the former. They had already created a list on the back of a heavy piece of paper.

Millie leaned over to whisper, "That was today's menu. In the absence of anyone else, I took the liberty of assisting them in revising it. I have, I am sad to say, some experience along that line."

"You did what was right." Georgia switched to French. "It will be a day of sandwiches and soup. Of a buffet kept fresh for Anne and her guests to eat as they feel able. And wine."

Monsieur Chouinard glanced up from the neat lines on his paper. "Of course, madame. You may leave it to us."

"Has the doctor been sent for?" she asked.

"Almost as soon as I was told," he said with some dignity. "The mayor of the town, who is also the family attorney, will have been informed. The priest will arrive at any moment, now that lauds are concluded. Would you be so kind as to receive him?"

"Yes, of course. In the drawing room?"

"*Oui, madame.*"

Madame Laurent followed them to the bottom of the service stairs. She clutched a handkerchief that Georgia could see was damp. "Madame, would you do us the kindness of conveying our sincere condolences to *la vicomtesse*? It would not be suitable for me to disturb her in her grief, but I feel it would help if she knew the staff feel every sympathy for her and the children at this time."

Georgia touched her arm in gratitude, but was not surprised when the dignified woman straightened so that Georgia's hand fell away. "I will be sure to tell her, madame. Thank you. I hope the day will not be too difficult for you."

"Easier in some ways, more difficult in others," she said. She bobbed a curtsey and turned away.

"Madame," Millie said hastily, "is there anything we should know about the priest and the church before we go up?"

Madame Laurent looked slightly puzzled, but answered readily enough. "He is Père Francois Laurent, and he has been in the service of the church for three years."

"Is he a relation?" Millie asked.

"My husband's cousin's son. The apple of his mother's eye and spoiled rotten. There was no one more surprised than I when he chose to take orders. However, he seems to have settled into his duties. I believe it has been the making of him."

Georgia had not heard the woman make such a long speech before. Garrulous she certainly was not, but evidently a little family pride could warm her into civility.

"*Merci, madame,*" Millie said in her perfect Parisian French. "Will you send up some *café au lait?*"

The other woman curtseyed again, and they climbed the steep stairs, grateful for the electricks that illuminated them and left hands free to manage skirts and banisters.

They found the young priest in the drawing room, gazing out the window toward the sea, hands clasped behind his back. The sky had lightened into the grey of the predawn. After introductions and the arrival of coffee, which Georgia felt so grateful for she could have wept, she invited him to be seated where the geologists had been last night.

"I am desolated at this news," the young man said sadly. His hair was cropped short, but given another inch or two, it would have been a riot of glossy dark curls. His eyes were brown and full of sorrow in a face tanned from the sun. "I should have liked to speak with him one last time—to continue our conversation from last night, at the party. He was an educated man—far more than I—but he never held it against me. He enjoyed debating doctrine as much as I enjoyed defending it."

"I am glad you had such a friendship," Georgia said. "He seems to have been universally liked by the staff."

"By everyone," Père Francois said frankly. "There will be much distress in the town, and beyond, when the news gets out. His holdings are extensive. This chateau is only one of three properties the family owns. The other two are smaller houses, but are situated among vineyards and large farms with several tenants."

He must be on intimate terms with the family to know so much.

He sipped his coffee and put the large white cup down in the saucer with a *clink*. "If it is convenient for *la vicomtesse*, I recommend we hold the service on Wednesday. That will allow family members to be notified and to travel. Luckily, the trains are reliable for those who do not come by air."

"That seems very fast," Millie said.

"We are in the south, madame," he said with a sad smile. "Please inform *la vicomtesse* I will make the arrangements for the funeral mass Wednesday morning at eleven in the de Valmy chapel, with the interment to follow in the family vault."

"I did not notice a cemetery as we landed," Millie said in some surprise. "Not even next to the church. Is it very small?"

"No, indeed, madame. It has been in existence for six centuries. The vault is below ground, in catacombs cut from the stone on which the estate sits. Anyone who lives in the de Valmy *demesne* is entitled to be buried there."

"Goodness me." Millie seemed to have forgotten the cup she held. "I have heard of the catacombs in Paris and Rome, but not in the country, in use by ordinary people."

"It is highly practical," he told her. "The air is very dry, which lends itself to preservation. During Napoleon's rule, people took refuge in them from the cannonbombs dropped by the airships of war."

"Let us hope we will not have to deal with that, at least," Georgia said firmly, offering to pour a second cup to her companions. "I trust there is an inn close by to house those who travel?"

"Yes, there are two in Valmy town, which will no doubt be sufficient. The family is scattered and there are not many of them." He declined a second cup. "Hence Gregory Campbell's accession to the title. The attorneys had to climb a fair distance into the family tree's branches to find the proper heir."

"You seem to know them very well," Millie observed.

"I grew up here," he said simply. "My father is the other attorney in town, and I was an altar boy at Notre Dame d'Esperance. I worked here as well, helping in the gardens until my father's cousin and his wife came."

Georgia was having a difficult time reconciling this gentle, intelligent young man with the spoiled brat she had heard of. Ah well, most people grew up eventually. And he did seem very comfortable with his calling.

"Perhaps you would be the appropriate person to notify his relations, then? We will inform Madame Fleury so that she may send a tube to her family."

"I should be happy to." He rose and bowed. "I had best begin making the arrangements. There is a lot to do, and we never have as much time as we would like. May I offer my condolences to *la vicomtesse* in person?"

"She was sleeping when we left her," Georgia said. "To be frank, I believe sleep is the best thing for her just now. May we send for you later, when she is ready to receive visitors?"

"I would be glad of that. Please let her know the sextons and I will come for *le vicomte* about midmorning. He will lie in the chapel until Wednesday." With a bow, he took his leave.

When Georgia returned from seeing him out, she sat

down with a sigh. "It is such a relief to feel one is not left to shoulder such arrangements alone."

"Yes," Millie said absently. "Goodness, the doctor has been an age. Perhaps we ought to go up and see if there has been some difficulty."

"Let me take him some café au lait."

She carried a cup and saucer up to *le vicomte*'s room. Millie peeked in on Anne through her dressing room door, and reported in a whisper, "Still asleep."

"Good. Let us give her as long as we can."

They found the doctor gently pulling up a sheet over Gregory Campbell's face. Though they did not make much noise, he turned as they came in.

"*Ah, merci,*" he said in a low voice, accepting the cooling coffee and downing it in a couple of gulps.

Georgia set the empty cup on a spindly table. "Your examination is complete?"

"*Oui.* I will not distress a lady with the details, however."

"If there is something *la vicomtesse* should know," Georgia said, "you may share it with us. We have … some experience."

He gazed at her a moment, as though debating whether or not to ask the nature of her experience, then gave a very Gallic shrug. "*Alors*, I have been searching for some clue as to the cause of death, but I may simply have to settle for the obvious. A heart attack. Were you with him earlier last night?"

"Yes, at dinner," Millie said.

"And did he seem all right then?"

"No," Georgia told him. "He was trembling when dinner was announced and we left the terrace. By the end of the first course I noticed his pupils were dilated. He was unable to finish his meal, and was helped upstairs by Comtesse de

Valmy and a distant relation of his, Monsieur Roger Campbell, who is staying here."

"I must say, you are very observant, madame."

"I was concerned. It tends to make one observant."

"Spoken like a mother," Millie said with a small smile. "I did see that his distress seemed to increase as each course came in."

"He did not eat something that might have caused choking?"

"No," Millie said. "He did not choke. And we all ate exactly the same thing with no ill effects. Except that I declined the duck. It is too rich for me."

Georgia told him what had been on the menu, and he shook his head. "Nothing that any of us have not eaten many times. Perhaps a mushroom in a sauce was confused with a poisonous one?"

After a moment of consideration, Georgia shook her head. "I do not recall mushrooms being served or in a sauce. When we were at school together, I remember *la comtesse* avoided them. Perhaps they still disagree with her, and Madame Laurent does not prepare them."

"It is worth looking into," Millie said. "I will ask her."

"I suspect you will find her ladyship here is in the right," Dr Besson said. He sighed as he gazed at the bed. "When will they come for him?"

"Midmorning," Georgia replied.

He nodded, as though he had suspected as much. "Thank you for answering my questions. I am not satisfied, but I have no evidence with which to inconvenience the magistrate and —oh." He blinked.

"Monsieur?" Georgia prompted, when he did not go on.

"*Le vicomte* was the magistrate." He scrubbed his face with one hand. "I suppose another will have to be appointed now. It makes an inquest rather difficult, had I wished to call one."

"Should the gendarmes be informed?" Millie asked. "And the magistrate, too, when he is appointed?"

"For what reason?" He collected his bag from the floor beside the bed. "No crime has been committed. And even if one had, would you subject *la vicomtesse* to their intrusion and questioning?"

"If a crime had been committed, *la vicomtesse* would be the first one to insist upon an investigation," Georgia said. "She has very clear ideas of right and wrong."

"That may be, but I cannot find a crime here. Just the loss of a man I respected, in sudden and most unfortunate circumstances."

His grief was clear in his distressed eyes and slumped shoulders. There seemed nothing more to do but see him downstairs to his small, battered steam landau and watch him out of sight.

CHAPTER FIVE

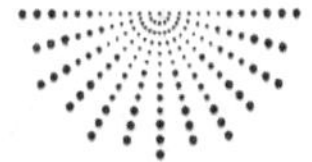

WEDNESDAY, MAY 29 AT 11:00 A.M

What a difference one saw in a community's mourning when the departed was liked and respected, and not feared and despised. Millie had been to a number of funerals—the most recent only weeks ago in Venice—but she compared this one with that of her nephew and Georgia's late husband Hartford, fourth Baron Langford.

In point of fact, there was no comparison.

The de Valmy chapel was packed so tightly that the choir had to stand on the balcony that had once been used by medieval ladies who did not wish to be gawked at by the people. There were no pews in use here; everyone stood, with the exception of *la vicomtesse,* whose Scottish fortitude had failed her utterly and who required a chair. Georgia and Millie, who would have stood with her to bear her up, had been gently crowded out of the way by Manon Fleury and the geologists, whose claims of blood apparently outranked those of love and friendship.

Millie suspected that they had been told of the parts she and Georgia had played while everyone was asleep in the small hours of Monday, and were rather put out about not having been included.

The service was longer than an English funeral. Millie pitied *le vicomte*'s little girls, wearing sober black dresses and hats with veils down to their shoulders, on either side of their mother's chair like small bookends.

Georgia, standing next to Millie toward the front, always looked very well in black, which had likely gone over nearly as badly with Manon and the others as any interference of which they thought her guilty.

After the final hymn, the procession formed. Millie took Georgia's arm, though normally she did not require such support. "Do not lose me," she begged in a whisper. She was not looking forward to the catacombs.

"I was just about to ask you the same thing," Georgia whispered back. "Buck up. If Anne can bear it, we can."

Gregory Campbell's coffin sat upon an apparatus comprising a bier with two large wheels on either side, and a small steam engine to propel it that it could be gently guided with one hand. The family walked directly behind the bier, with Georgia, Millie, the doctor, the neighbors, and all the village following behind in a long, snaking procession.

Across the lawns they walked, through the wildflower meadows, and thence to a squat tower that Millie had not noticed when she and Georgia had come down here that first day. It was ancient—showing every day of the six centuries the priest had mentioned. A short ramp had long ago been cut down to the door, which was of blackened oak with iron hinges, and stood open. The sextons stood to either side, dressed in black. A narrow-gauge rail system began at the door, where the coffin was transferred from the rolling apparatus to one resembling a flat train car.

"It is a cablecar system, like those in the mines at Burg Salzweg," Georgia whispered to Millie. "They seem to have adapted it very cleverly to this sad use."

Millie tried to imagine how they must have done it in centuries past, without benefit of such technology. A very long walk with men trading off places carrying the coffin on their shoulders, no doubt. Old-fashioned moonglobes hung in iron baskets dangling from the low ceiling of the tunnel, forcing tall men like the doctor and Roger Campbell to duck every dozen feet or so.

The deeper underground they went, the more convoluted the tunnel became, the track dividing and having to be switched by the sextons at the head of the procession. The tunnel widened periodically to reveal galleries of horizontal apertures carved in the rock, each containing the remains of de Valmys and townspeople past. The de Valmy recesses were easily identified by the family crest of the deer and the hawk carved in the rock, with DUCAT QUI PACEM CUPIT nearly obliterated in the oldest by time and the hands of passing mourners.

"He who desireth peace leadeth," Millie translated. "I wonder how that was received during the Crusades ... or the Napoleonic Wars, for that matter?"

"I am sure there is someone here who can tell you," Georgia said under her breath. "But we must be silent now."

She was right. No one spoke. Or sang, or even prayed. Only the soft weeping of Anne and her girls could be heard above the shuffle of hundreds of feet and the clank of the cables under the track.

At length they arrived in a gallery that looked somewhat less ancient than the ones they had passed. Millie had no idea where they were under the de Valmy grassy acres. They could be two hundred feet out under the seabed, for all she knew, like the mines in Cornwall. She and Georgia stood respectfully as the coffin was hoisted off the car and into its designated niche, which had already been neatly carved with Gregory's name and the dates of his birth and death.

When the sextons lowered their arms, someone back in the tunnel began to sing. Millie's very hair stood on end, so haunting and mournful was the tune, so unexpected in the utter silence. After the first line, sung in a Provençal dialect that was probably as ancient as this place, the townsfolk joined in. Even Manon, who did not live here, knew the words.

But in this way poor Gregory was honored, and joined the ranks of his family going back many generations, for his final rest.

When the last tremulous notes died away, the muted rustle of footsteps resumed. Fifteen minutes later, Millie and Georgia emerged into the warmth and the sunlight, and it was all Millie could do not to fall to her knees in the poppies and give thanks for her deliverance from the closeness and the dark. When she turned respectfully to allow Anne to pass, it was to see her and the twins riding upon the rolling apparatus, their feet neatly tucked up under their skirts, backs straight, their bodies swaying as the wheels negotiated the wide path.

Anne did not look at them as she was borne past. Millie could only be grateful that the poor woman did not have to walk all that way back to the chateau. A funeral was a solemn ceremony, but at least here, among these country burial customs, someone had had the goodness to think of the bereaved.

LA VICOMTESSE RETURNED to her room, and the governess abstracted Elodie and Eloise from the mourners and spirited them upstairs as well. Once again, as the lady of highest rank present, Georgia found herself in collusion with Monsieur Chouinard the butler, Madame Laurent, and the staff to preside over luncheon and to see that the family and the townsfolk did justice to de Valmy by consuming the very considerable spread. What miracles Madame had worked in the scant two days she'd had to prepare! Sliced meats of every description, terrines and salads in jewel hues, and pyramids of fruit, rolls, and complicated pastries that Georgia could not even identify, but which were delicious.

Her respect for the woman grew until even she had to admit that she would not have sacked her, either, cleavers notwithstanding.

By sunset, the only guests remaining were members of the family who had come from various corners of France, and who would not make the return journey until tomorrow. They were sixteen to dinner, including the geologists and the Villiers, Dr Besson, and the priest. Stefan and his wife sat opposite Georgia, who could not bring herself to sit in Anne's place, but resumed her seat at the right hand of the missing head of the house.

"I must thank you, Monsieur Villiers, for your help on that unfortunate night," she said over her cassoulet. "When one is in unfamiliar surroundings, the presence of friends who know what to do is comforting."

"You do not give the impression of not knowing what to do, madame," he said. "I thought all went very well today."

"I just answered questions and everyone else did the work," she admitted. "From Père Francois to the kitchen maids, everyone has been a credit to de Valmy and the family."

"Have you heard from *monsieur l'avocat* regarding the will?"

Perhaps customs were different in France, and the neighbors felt free to discuss matters in public which were decidedly private in England. Georgia opened her mouth to reply in the negative, though Père Francois had pointed out his father to her in the crowd today.

"Oh, that won't pose any difficulty," Sibyl said, spooning up cassoulet as if she hadn't eaten a loaded plate earlier. "My brother is the heir."

Georgia was so surprised she could only blink. "Your brother? Roger?"

"Why, yes. I thought you knew—they are cousins."

"In France, madame, these things are decided by the court," Stefan Villiers put in, amusement glimmering at the corners of his mouth. "The ownership of an estate as old as de Valmy cannot be decided by fiat. The Court of Inheritance in Aix-en-Provence keeps all the old patents and coats of arms, and tracks the family trees with great precision. They are the ones who discovered that Gregory was the actual heir, not several candidates here in France who believed themselves about to accede to that honor." He glanced down the table, but Georgia could not be certain who he was looking at. Manon Fleury sat between a couple from Grenoble and an elderly gentleman from Nice.

"I don't believe you," Sibyl said flatly. She looked into her cassoulet as if to assure herself it was empty, then laid down her fork. "Court or no court, he is Gregory's closest relative."

"That may be so, madame, but the court will ascertain it. *L'avocat*—Monsieur Laurent the attorney, you understand—must necessarily be informed of their ruling before he reads the will."

"And how long will that take?" Roger Campbell finally seemed to apprehend the gist of the conversation.

Stefan lifted a shoulder. "I do not know. It took some months before they settled on and located your cousin. But since they found him, I suppose a subsequent search will not be so difficult. They have a more recent starting point, you see."

"Let's hope it doesn't," Sibyl said. "Though I wish to condole with dear Anne, of course, it is difficult now that our cousin is gone. I expected the estate would be settled within a week."

The sooner these two were out of Anne's hair, the better, as far as Georgia was concerned. "Perhaps it may."

"How long will you and your aunt be staying?" Roger asked her. "For there are no family matters to concern you."

How gauche he was. Beside him, Millie straightened her spine and addressed a polite question to Père Francois on her other side.

"As long as Anne wishes us to remain," Georgia said with a benevolent smile. "We have already moved back aboard *Helena*, as our rooms were needed by *le vicomte*'s other relations and guests." Ever so gently, she stressed the word *other*. "There were so few that I insisted they stay here, rather than in an inn."

"You are quite the lady of the house," Sibyl observed. "How grateful Anne must be that she doesn't have to think of a thing."

"I have some experience both in the management of a large household and in bereavement," Georgia said rather more briefly than politeness required. She turned to Manon, sitting two places down. "Is your family waiting for you in Nantes still? When does your ship lift?"

"In two days," she said. "But we will not be on it."

"Whyever not?" Georgia's tone held her surprise.

"Because, *chere madame*, my eldest son is one of those at whom the Court of Inheritance will be looking."

"I beg your pardon?" Sibyl leaned slightly over her cassoulet dish, making it difficult for the footman to extract it. "Why should that be?"

"We, too, are related to de Valmy," she said calmly. "And my son has the distinction of being the only boy born to this generation of our branch of the family. My husband and I both felt it was more important to remain and hear of his fate than to travel so far, only to return if the court ruled in his favor."

"Bless us," Sibyl said. "Roger, did you hear that? Is everyone here related to our cousin?"

"I am not," Georgia said.

"Nor am I," Stefan told her. "I have an interest in the estate, however."

"An interest, monsieur?" Manon inquired. She sounded rather chilly, as though he had hinted *le vicomte* had lost some portion of the estate in a gambling debt.

"*Oui.* Our estates, as you know, march together on one boundary. That boundary passes through two rivers and part of the canal system in this part of the country. Rights to that water and the control of it became increasingly important as both de Valmy and I expanded our agricultural interests."

"What does all that mean, sir?" Sibyl said impatiently. "What has that got to do with the heir to the estate?"

"I expect he will want to come to some sort of legal agreement as to the rights," Millie said calmly. "And that can only be done with the owner of the property. Is it not so, monsieur?"

Stefan smiled at her. "You are quite right, madame. Do you have experience in such matters?"

"Indeed not." Millie smiled back, and included his silent wife in her smile. "But I am very interested in gardens, which do not survive without water. I expect rice, cabbage, and even lavender are the same."

Stefan chuckled. "They are, madame. And most lucrative they are, too."

But Sibyl was not finished. "So everyone at this table has an interest in who inherits the de Valmy estates? Except Lady Langford and Miss Brunel, of course."

Georgia signaled to the footman with one eyebrow that several wine glasses were empty. "I feel that one very important fact is missing from this discussion. Manon, you may take to the air tomorrow as planned and enjoy your voyage. Mr and Miss Campbell, you may continue your tour of geological sites as soon as you wish. And *mesdames et messieurs,* honored relations of de Valmy, you may return home to wait for news as and when it pleases you. Because no decisions will be made as to who the heir might be until September."

Stefan smothered a smile with one hand, and accepted another glass of wine. Manon sat back in her chair as though her spine had given out, her face blank with the realization that clearly had not yet occurred to the rest of the guests.

"And what gives you the authority to say such a thing?" Sibyl snapped.

"Ridiculous woman, cease your prattle." A voice like the creaking of a wrought-iron gate carried down the length of the table. Sibyl gasped and turned toward the speaker, the woman of some considerable avoirdupois from Grenoble, who stared back with utter contempt in her dark eyes. "If you had a brain in your head, mademoiselle, you would know that no decisions can be made until *la vicomtesse* has had her baby. If she bears a son, none of you will inherit. And until that time, I am sure she would be grateful if all of you vultures would leave her in peace."

Thursday, May 30, at 8:15 a.m.

Millie and Georgia walked down the gravel avenue after a comfortable night aboard *Helena*, feeling the cool of the morning dissolving in the heat of the sun. Millie stopped to sniff the salmon-pink geraniums in one of the stone urns.

"I wonder who might still be here," she said in a low voice to Georgia. "Mr and Miss Campbell spent all of yesterday fossil-hunting, and did not even appear at dinner. The gentleman from Nice is gone, leaving only that terrifying woman from Grenoble, who I believe is in the room overlooking the rose garden."

"A shame you had to give it up," Georgia said sympathetically.

"I gave it up most willingly," Millie hastened to assure her as they continued on their way to breakfast. "At least aboard

Helena I am in no danger of being accosted by enraged heirs presumptive."

"Heirs presumptuous, you mean." Georgia sniffed in disdain. "What a lot of silly geese, not to know everything must pause until the baby is born."

"I would have expected Manon to have gone to join her family by now."

"I suppose we shall see. Millie, where are you going?"

Millie paused and looked back over her shoulder. "I will join you in a moment. I want to ask Madame Laurent if I may pick some ingredients for a tisane for *la vicomtesse*. The one I made for you after—" She stopped, reconsidered her next words. "After Helena left us."

A smile of comprehension warmed Georgia's face. "How considerate you are. I am sure it will help Anne as much as it helped me. I will hie me off to the breakfast room and hope it is too early for anyone else to be down."

Millie made her way across the neat forecourt to the ivy-covered wall that, to her best calculations, was the one surrounding the kitchen garden. She risked having a cleaver brandished at her for coming in the garden gate, she thought as she pushed its neatly painted wrought iron open, but it saved a lot of stairs and corridors just to come in directly. She would seek out Madame right away to secure her permission. And if she were caught without it, surely, as a guest, she could not be blamed for not knowing that entry was forbidden?

The gate closed behind her with a clang and she stopped to get her bearings. Goodness, the kitchen garden was at least an acre, maybe more, laid out in squares and rectangles of both raised and ground-level beds. Here were vegetables more numerous even than the garden at Langford Park, vigorous with early summer, as though each plant were anxious to get on with the business of bearing the harvest.

No flowers seemed permitted to waste the space until Millie's steps carried her past an ancient mulberry tree so old its boughs were held up by posts, a creamy glory of elderberry trees in full bloom next to it. Beyond was a riot of flowers, in a sunny corner against the rear wall upon which were espaliered apple and pear trees.

"So, Madame, you do have a weakness. What are your favorites tucked away back here? Is this where your mistress tried to plant her little lavender?"

She could see something with bells of blue, but was not close enough to identify it. She was about twenty feet away when someone shouted in a tone that sent Millie straight back to boarding school and made her stomach jump.

She dragged in a fortifying breath of air, scented with soil and the tang of tomato plants, and turned.

Madame Laurent was steaming toward her like a train into a station. "Mademoiselle Brunel!" she shouted. "Are you lost? No person but the kitchen maids and my husband is allowed in here."

"My deepest apologies, madame," Millie said. It was all she could do to keep her shoulders from hunching up around her ears. "The gate was unlocked … I did not know that guests were not to come in."

Madame rolled her eyes and huffed. "That Marie-Jeanne is always running out to see her beau and leaving the gate unlocked. I will have words with her." Her temper seemed to be cooling slightly, and to Millie's relief, she did not carry an implement of any kind. "You are the lady who enjoys the garden, yes?"

"Yes," Millie said, finding the Provençal dialect a little easier to understand the longer she heard it. "I have never seen one as lovely and large as this."

"It feeds all those in the chateau and some beyond," madame said in a mollified tone. "Please come into the house. It is too hot to be standing out here. Have you had your breakfast?"

"No, not yet." Somehow Millie found herself at the kitchen door when what she would have liked was a tour of the garden. But perhaps the chef was busy getting breakfast for the remaining guests, and had no time for dallying about identifying plants. "Perhaps sometime I might pick a few herbs and leaves? I should like to make a tisane for *la vicomtesse*. My niece found it very helpful on the unhappy occasion of her own bereavement."

"If you send a note listing what you need, I shall see them delivered to you, madame." Millie must be rising in her estimation indeed to be addressed as madame, not mademoiselle. "If you take this corridor and the first set of stairs, you will find yourself very near the breakfast room without having to use the servants' door."

"I—well, thank you—"

But Madame Laurent had already departed, bustling down the corridor at what appeared to be her habitual rate of speed. For a woman whose dignity seemed part of her person, she covered the ground quickly.

Chastened, she found the breakfast room just where madame had said it would be. Georgia stood alone at the buffet, considering her choices, a plate in one hand. "Back already?"

"Sadly, yes." Millie took a plate and what appeared to be a

little egg pie filled with herbs, onions, and bacon, and topped with a dollop of sour cream. She added creamed potatoes and a finely cut savory salad. Divine. "She chased me out, but at a businesslike walk. And no cleaver."

Georgia sat at the table and spread a snowy napkin on her lap. "She is certainly very protective of her garden."

Millie took the chair next to her. "There must be a great number of rare plants that cannot be replaced. Such a variety of vegetables as I've never seen, including what will be pumpkins and squashes, and fruit trees already ripening, including an ancient mulberry and three or four elderberry trees. Spring must come very early here."

"April, perhaps earlier."

"But I did discover that madame has a weakness for flowers. She has about a hundred square feet in a sunny corner that is a perfect riot of all different kinds. Even what might have been hollyhocks, though I was too far away to see clearly before I was apprehended."

"I thought those flowered later in the summer."

"Perhaps not here. Or they were something else. In any case, I should love to know what they are. I am half tempted to wait until market day tomorrow and then sneak back in to see."

Georgia laughed. "Millie, my dear, your career as lady in waiting to the Empress has given you far too many skills in deception."

"Airs far above my station, more likely," Millie admitted with no guilt at all. "But I have another reason for wanting to look at the garden."

Georgia had almost finished her egg pie. "And what is that? I know you have designs on the one at home."

"When I asked for the ingredients for my tisane, madame suggested I send down a list, and she would collect them for me. But half the pleasure of making it is picking the flowers and leaves."

Her niece simply shook her head. "Market day, my dear. No one will ever know, and I am willing to wager the staff will never tell."

CHAPTER SIX

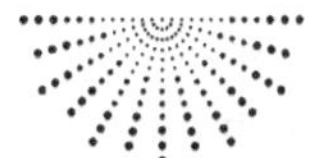

FRIDAY, MAY 31, AT 7:00 A.M.

The de Valmy airfield had the advantage not only of providing a direct route to the chateau, but of having one side bounded by the road leading to the market town two miles away. Millie had been up since daybreak, which meant that Georgia had, too. All this secrecy surrounding something as commonplace as picking leaves in a kitchen garden had set her antennae twitching. It might be nothing, of course. A cook was perfectly entitled to ward off tramping feet and careless hands when it came to fruit and vegetables she needed for the household.

But Georgia's ability to listen to her own intuition had been honed to a much finer point since their departure from England several weeks ago. Indeed, she had begun to feel she had been asleep all those years at Langford Park. Some of the time it had been on purpose, her mind avoiding a life that was unbearable. But that life was no more, thank goodness. Now she was awake, and interested in the world about her, and alert to small things like the beauty of flowers and the appeal of male voices and the deliciousness of lace and kisses … and the existence of facts that seemed slightly out of place.

Most things out of place had an explanation, no matter how banal. Finding it was, quite simply, satisfying.

"They are gone," Millie reported, coming to the door of Georgia's cabin. "Having neither basket nor scissors, I shall have to make do with my hands, if you will help me."

"Perhaps we will find gloves near the door with the sun hats," Georgia said. "I will fetch some and meet you at the gate in the wall."

But when she joined Millie with two hats and one pair of gloves, it was to find the gate locked, and too snug in its aperture to allow even a woman as slender as Millie to slip through. "We shall have to go through the kitchen," Millie said, "in full view of madame's staff. I don't much relish that."

"Never fear. I will handle them."

But Georgia did not need to play the lady of a manor not her own this morning. By some stroke of luck, it appeared as though the kitchen maids had gone with their mistress. From the butler's pantry came the clank of a tureen lid.

"Quick," Millie whispered. "Through that door over there."

Ten steps later, they were outside, with a stout door between them and discovery. At least until someone looked out of a window.

"It is completely unreasonable to feel so guilty," Georgia said, following Millie down the neatly kept paths to the elder trees and breathing their divine scent. "I would wonder if Anne knew of it, if she hadn't already told us the garden was forbidden to her, too."

"I shall put all the blame on you if we are discovered," Millie said, collecting several clusters of elderflower. "You are the only one who doesn't know. Can you find some lemon balm? One stem of nice leaves should be more than enough."

"How do I know lemon balm from licorice?"

"It smells like lemon." Millie waved a hand. "The herb beds are over there, closer to the kitchen door."

Georgia did as she was told, and collected a stem or two of mint while she was at it. Mint tea was also refreshing to the spirit. Perhaps if Anne did not care for it, they might make it aboard *Helena*. If they possessed a teapot. Perhaps she had better check. If not, she would make a delightful excursion into the town to find one.

Along with the elderflowers, Millie now had a small collection of leaves. "Thank you—these are all we need. I shall steep them in hot water and take it up to Anne with a tray of breakfast. But first, I must have a peek at that flower garden."

It looked like an ordinary flower garden to Georgia—not even laid out in a checkered pattern like the red and green lettuces, or in a pretty spiral like the parsley and chives, curving around each other. It was just a tumble of flowers, blue and purple, with the occasional accent of white. In the far corner, a couple of oleander bushes were a foam of pink and red, lending an accent. In terracotta pots against the wall where the pear trees left off were bushes of some kind, bearing pendulous yellow trumpets just beginning to open.

The flowers seemed riotously healthy, the spires of blue tall and thick. "Why, these are monkshood, Millie. They grow in the gardens at home." She was just reaching out to pick one of the stems when Millie gasped.

"Don't touch it, Georgia," she said urgently. "Don't touch any of them."

"I am not afraid of Madame Laurent," she assured her. "We

have already settled that I didn't know this garden was forbidden."

"Now I know why. Dearest—this is a poison garden."

All desire to touch anything faded and Georgia looked down at the aromatic herb in her hand. "What? This mint is not poison." At least she hoped not. "Nor are those pears, or those carrots. What do you mean?"

"Not the garden in general. This corner. I would wager that *la vicomtesse* was coming over here to plant her lavender so that it would not be seen, and madame caught her digging in it. Georgia, every plant in this plot is poisonous." She pointed. "What you called monkshood is also known as wolfsbane—it is deadly. And there. Oleander can kill in seven minutes. And those lovely golden blossoms—Angel's Trumpet. They will make you terribly sick."

Georgia stared at her. "How on earth do you know this? Have you been raiding the library here already?"

"No indeed. There has been no time for leisure pursuits. Do you remember when I represented the empress at the Medicinal Garden in Munich? They were so pleased at my interest that they showed me all over it, including the poison garden. They use the plants in that particular case to train young doctors to identify symptoms."

"I did not realize poison was used so regularly in Munich."

"Do not mock me."

"I was not, truly." Georgia touched her arm, and then gripped it, creasing the delicate white voile, as a thought struck her. "Millie, for heaven's sweet sake. You don't think—"

"I have absolutely no right to think anything. No training. No experience in such matters." She covered Georgia's hand on her arm with her own cold one. "But Doctor Besson did not understand why a healthy man should die of a heart attack so very suddenly."

"That was why he maintained for so long that it had to have been indigestion," Georgia said, trying to put in order the terrible events of last Sunday evening. "Because Gregory had no reason to die of a heart attack."

"Unless it was induced somehow." Millie gazed at the lovely blue spires of the monkshood swaying in the sunshine. They clung to one another as though each were a bulwark in a sudden storm.

"Millie, I cannot bear it. That kind man. The love of Anne's life. How could—how could anyone—?"

"We do not know that anyone has. It is madness even to think of it."

But what was murder but a form of madness? A moment's loss of control, changing lives forever. Or even a more deliberate series of actions, prompted less by hot passion than cold rage, but equally mad in its very calculation.

"I cannot bear to think of it. We have no proof, and the dear man is already in his tomb. Unlike Sir Francis Thorne, whose body bore evidence of an attack, Doctor Besson did not mention any such thing in this case."

"He would have told you?"

"He was so offended at our insistence he was wrong, I am not certain he would have offered up any further evidence to prove it."

Millie did not seem inclined to let go of Georgia's hand, either because she needed the comfort, or because she thought Georgia still might be tempted to pick something out of the poison garden. "Would you think me mad if I examined this flowerbed more closely?"

"If we were not wearing sun hats and frightened out of our wits, I would think us both mad. What are you looking for?" Georgia released her.

Millie walked around the poison garden until she found a stick. "I would put this off, but who knows when the next market day will be? Luckily we are screened a little by that mulberry tree."

"Put what off?" Millie bent to probe among the flowers. "Millie, tell me."

"I am looking for a broken stem, or perhaps some disturbed soil where something has been dug up. It may mean nothing. Or…"

Or it might mean something. Exactly what, Georgia was not prepared to say out loud.

Ten minutes passed in which Georgia decided she would be more useful standing watch than supervising. But no shadows watched them from the mullioned windows. Nothing moved in the kitchen garden but butterflies, birds, and bees sailing to their hives along the far wall where the gate was.

And Millie's careful parting of stems and stooped examinations. "Oh, no." Millie exhaled. "Come look at this."

Georgia joined her, leaning in while, with her stick, Millie parted the monkshood plants toward the middle of the plot. Among the plants, the soil was disturbed, crumbled around a small depression where a plant had been. Millie's stick was withdrawn, and the surrounding plants' leaves and flowers closed ranks to conceal the presence of the hole.

Simultaneously, Georgia's keen hearing detected the rattle of the market wagon returning with the Laurents and the two kitchen maids. "We must go," she said urgently. "The gate!"

"No, not that way—Marie-Jeanne is with them. We will not be able to blame its being unlocked on her. Hurry!"

The two of them dashed down the neat grassy paths to the kitchen. They had only seconds before madame came in from the walled stableyard. Even now they could hear the guttural whistle of the wagon's steam engine as the pressure was released.

A footman appeared in the doorway of the butler's pantry and practically dropped the tray of scones and jam he was holding. "Mesdames—!"

"*Bonjour!*" Millie sang as they hurried down the corridor so fast it was almost a run. "It is nothing. *Merci.*"

They ran up the steps and through the door near the breakfast room. But they couldn't talk there. Georgia opened the nearest door, which turned out to be Gregory's study. Gasping, she pulled Millie inside, closed the door, and leaned on it as though an army were about to storm it from the other side.

Millie opened her hands to reveal the elderflowers and other herbs she had collected. The scents of mint and lemon rose in the air. "I am sure a little crushing will not hurt their effectiveness."

"I am sure it won't, if it's all about to be boiled. Millie, what did you mean back there, when you said *oh no?*"

"The entire plant was gone."

"Yes, I saw. But I cannot think why anyone would dig up a poisonous plant so carefully. To transplant it? Where?"

"They told me, at the Medicinal Garden, that the poison of monkshood is strongest in the root. No portion of the root had been left behind that I could see."

Georgia was almost afraid to ask. "And what does the root do to a person?"

"We must find out. Immediately. Because if it produces the same symptoms as a heart attack, *le vicomte*'s was not an unexpected death."

No. It had been with malice aforethought.

THEY COULD NOT ASK Madame Laurent to brew the tea with stolen herbs, so while Georgia went up to Anne, Millie hurried down the avenue to *Helena*. In their few delightful days of outfitting the ship, surely they must have put a teapot somewhere.

But they had not. Clearly the Continent had affected their habits if a single day could pass without tea! She would just have to make do.

With a little of the water in the boiler siphoned off into a copper kettle, she popped the herbs in, and from the scent, their rough handling had not harmed them. She found a large drinking glass and poured the steaming brew into it, then wrapped it in a towel and took it down to the chateau.

She found Georgia and Anne curled up in the sunny window seat in Anne's room like a pair of schoolgirls. But when Anne turned to accept the warm tisane, the merry woman who had welcomed them on Sunday had gone. Perhaps forever.

"Thank you, Millie." She sipped. "Georgia tells me you dosed her with this after she was widowed."

"I did. Every day. Did Georgia tell you how we came by the ingredients today?"

Anne's mouth curved in a smile, then fell. "The mark of true friendship is braving a cleaver to help a friend."

"We did no such thing," Georgia said. "We waited until she went to the market."

"How many days must I drink it?"

"I made a good amount—three days' worth."

"If I find it helpful, you must write out the recipe and my lady's maid can make it for me. Mind you, Madame D will have to pick the ingredients. I do not wish poor Hortense to lose a hand pinching elderflowers in my service."

It had not occurred to Millie that Anne would want to continue taking the tisane. For until they discovered what the symptoms of monkshood were, how it had been administered, and then who might have hated the poor *vicomte* enough to kill him, anyone who could walk into the kitchen garden, by day or night, was suspect.

Someone could easily squeeze a few drops of monkshood juice into a cup of tisane and that would put paid to the unborn heir.

"I am certain that three days will see you feeling better, madame," Millie said at last.

Georgia opened her mouth, no doubt to mention how many days Millie had made it for her. Millie flashed a warning in her eyes, and Georgia closed her lips.

"Please call me Anne," *la vicomtesse* said, sipping the tisane. "And I shall call you Millie, if you permit it."

"Of course, Anne," Millie said warmly. "How are your little girls bearing up?"

"Better than I. Their governess believes that a course of botany is just the thing at the moment, so they are haring about the meadows learning the names of wildflowers and identifying shells down on the beach, far from the gloom of the house."

"Your governess is a treasure," Georgia said. "I would prescribe the same for you if it were not impertinent."

Anne snorted. "As if that would ever stop you."

"Perhaps it would do you good to walk up and see our little ship," Georgia persisted. "Tomorrow? You can drink your tisane with us."

"I apologize for the drinking glass," Millie said. "We have no teapot."

Anne straightened. "No teapot? Why, that is simply barbaric. You must rectify that at once with a trip into Valmy."

"Only if you are our guide." Georgia leaped in where Millie feared to tread. "Yes, you will have to face those who would offer condolences, and it will be awful, but you must show your face sometime."

"It would be best for the girls if *maman* were to take up the reins of life and return it to some semblance of normalcy," Millie said gently.

Anne shook her head. "Neither of you know how it is here. It is the custom to observe six months of deep mourning." She put down the empty glass on the wide windowsill with a *clack.* "Do not harangue me."

"I apologize, dearest," Georgia said, flushing. "Forgive us."

Now it was Anne's turn to redden. "How could you know? And I am abundantly not myself. If I walk up to your *Helena* now, will you forgive me? At least it is on the grounds, and I am wearing enough black to satisfy any stickler."

"Gladly." Georgia picked up the glass. "Did I tell you we were sleeping aboard so that the relatives could have our rooms?"

Anne stopped halfway across the carpet. "You cannot be serious. The chateau has rooms enough for all of them and more."

"It is no trouble," Millie said. "We quite like it. Anne—you do not mind if I pop into the library? I will catch you up. I should like to find a book to help me sleep in times when my mind is troubled."

"Of course. Please consider the house your own. The library is directly below us, so it is easy to find."

"I confess I have been directing your staff these past few days," Georgia said, linking arms with Anne and walking down the stairs with her. Their voices faded as they went out the door, while Millie lost no time in locating the library. She hoped very much that someone in the family besides the children had an interest in botany.

To her surprise, it was already occupied by the two girls and their governess.

"I do beg your pardon, mesdemoiselles," Millie said, feeling as though she had been caught stealing. "*La vicomtesse* assured me I might choose a book."

"Of course, Miss Brunel," Elodie—she was quite sure it was Elodie—said in English with just a touch of a Scottish roll on the *R*. "We are identifying wildflowers, but this book is too large to take with us."

"That is just what I have come to do," Millie said with a smile. "Can you point me to the section that book came from?"

"Perhaps the flower you are looking for is in here?" Eloise tilted up the book—the size of an atlas, with a painted plate of some kind of lily on one side of the spread and a lengthy description on the other. "Do you know its name?"

Now was the time to slip on her dotty grandmother persona. "I am afraid not—but it is very pretty—tall, with spires of drooping blue flowers."

"Oh, we just saw something like that." Elodie flipped pages. "This one?"

"No, not a hollyhock. A lighter blue."

"Phlox!" Eloise said. "But *non* ... that is an ordinary garden flower, not a wildflower. A bluebell, perhaps?"

"No, it is much taller," Millie said, holding out a hand at hip height. "The flowers look like little people wearing hoods."

"Monkshood, madame?" The governess's brows rose. "You find these in the meadows here?"

"I thought I saw one," she said uncertainly. "There, have you found it?"

"If it is out in the meadow, we will pull it up," the governess said. "*Voyons*, what does it say?"

The girls took turns reading the description, then soon tired of stamens and sepals. "Miss Brunel, this is a dangerous plant," Elodie said, her finger dropping lower. "Listen—I will translate."

Millie took the liberty of standing just close enough to pretend to look at the beautifully painted monkshood spire while rapidly scanning the lines of academic French as the little girl read aloud.

"*Aconitum napellus is poisonous in all its parts, including leaves, flowers, and root. The toxin may be absorbed through the skin simply by picking the flowers or leaves ungloved. The juice of the root is particularly dangerous, resulting in death within—*"

"Elodie, that is enough." Her governess clapped the book closed. "It is not good for you to read of death, *cherie*. There has been enough of that already."

"But Miss Brunel—"

"I am sure Miss Brunel agrees with me."

Millie hastened to assure her that she did, having read swiftly to the end of the passage. "Forgive me if I have brought your father's passing back to mind when you were so pleasantly occupied. You are a very good translator, Elodie."

"Eloise is, too," the girl said. "Would you like to take the book away with you?"

"That is quite all right. You have educated me sufficiently that I shall give the plant a wide berth. And none of us will be pulling it up, will we?"

The girls shook their heads in a solemn promise and Millie took her leave.

Evidently the gentleman leading the tour at the Medicinal Garden had watered down his remarks out of consideration for her feminine sensibilities. The words that Elodie had *not* read were now imprinted on Millie's memory. No one could forget words as terrible as these.

The juice of the root is particularly dangerous, in some cases resulting in death within an hour of ingestion, within eight hours in others. The mouth may feel burning or numbness, as may the stomach. Weakness in the limbs signals the next stage, followed by difficulty breathing and an uneven pulse. The heart may struggle for some minutes, but eventually must succumb in death, often giving the appearance of a heart attack. There is no antidote yet discovered, and this author deplores the common propagation of Aconitum napellus in all too many gardens.

CHAPTER SEVEN

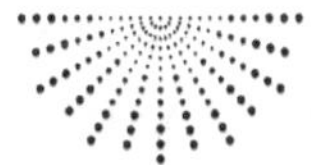

eorgia and Anne concluded their tour of *Helena* in
the communications cage, where, in a pigeon with
the *Foresight* crest engraved on its gleaming brass
side, a fat letter waited. She slipped it into her pocket and
turned to find Anne gazing at her expectantly.

"A letter from Teddy?"

Oh, why did the heat have to prickle into her face now,
under that grey gaze from which she had never been able to
hide a single thing? "No. From a friend."

Anne was clearly trying not to smile. "A verbose friend."

Georgia gave up. "A male friend, if you must know. A
maddening, absent, frighteningly intelligent, secretive friend
whom I would cut dead if I weren't so wretchedly attracted to
him."

Anne practically dragged her into the saloon, where the
sun fell in ovals through its large viewing ports. "Tell all," she
commanded, seating herself on the sofa. "I must think about
something with a little joy in it."

So Georgia did, at some length. Millie joined them in time

to hear Mr van Meere's name, at which her blush told the same truth as Georgia's. Honestly, it was a good thing neither of them planned a life of crime. They would be abject failures at it. Even at Burg Salzweg, despite all Millie's practice, they hadn't been able to pull off an impersonation for the length of an afternoon.

"Georgia, I am so glad," Anne said on a sigh. "While I understand your doubts about proceeding faster … or even farther … I am delighted that you are receiving the attentions of someone who may just be your equal."

"It is too soon to say." The heavy envelope in her pocket felt like a promise to both herself and Millie. She pulled it out and handed it to her companion. "This was waiting for us."

Millie's smile as she read the direction took twenty years off her face. This was the Millie who should have been, all these years. A Millie who was appreciated, respected, loved, with her own household and family. And while Georgia certainly respected and loved her, Millie's receiving such gifts from a man she esteemed was a very different thing from those of a female companion. She only hoped Mr van Meere realized what a treasure he was courting.

Of Mr Seacombe, she was not prepared to conjecture further. For all she knew, he had included a note bearing six lines, mostly concerning the weather.

When Millie looked up, her delight had faded, as though less pleasant thoughts had returned to cloud her prospects.

"Did you find what you were looking for in the library?" Anne asked.

Millie flashed a glance at Georgia before replying. "I did, thank you. I found the girls and their governess there, too, studying a book of wildflowers, which was just what I had been looking for." She gave a self-deprecating smile. "I am a bit of a gardener, and appreciate a good espalier as much as anyone, but the charm of wildflowers is irresistible."

"Indeed," Anne said. "Not what I would choose for bedtime reading, but I am glad you found something. Were the girls trying to identify a plant?"

"Yes, a lily of some sort."

"And you?" Georgia asked quietly.

"I did as well. It was exactly as I thought."

A chill landed in Georgia's stomach like a stone in a pond, horror rippling outward in waves.

"Georgia, goodness, you look as if you've seen a ghost." Anne peered out the viewing port as though something out of doors might have alarmed her.

Oh dear. They had stepped in it now. She didn't know whether to fabricate a story or to simply tell the truth. But her years of living with Hartford Brunel had taught her the value of truth. She would not demean Anne's quick mind and loving heart with a lie, no matter how well meant.

"I suppose I have," she said slowly. "Oh, Anne, I can't bring myself to spoil our lovely afternoon with some dreadful suspicions."

Anne pushed herself upright in alarm. "You've done the job famously now. Out with it, my girl."

Millie stepped into the breach like the brave woman she was. "In my recent education about plants, I have been interested in those that heal, and … those that harm. The plant I learned about today, thanks to the book your girls were studying, was *Aconitum napellus.* Monkshood."

Anne gazed at her as though she really was the dotty old

woman she sometimes pretended to be. "Monkshood? Isn't that rather too common for study?"

"The doctor who attended your husband was distressed when his initial diagnosis of indigestion proved instead to be a heart attack," Millie went on steadily. "He could not understand how a man in excellent health, with no history of heart ailments, could have succumbed so quickly to so strong an attack."

"He is not the only one," Anne said, her mouth grim.

"In my brief study of the properties of monkshood just now, I learned that the root, and in particular its juice, when administered to a human being, produces first numbness in the mouth, then weakness in the limbs, then a heartbeat so uneven that eventually, after some struggle, it … ceases altogether."

The color drained out of Anne's face and Georgia reached for her. "Millie, some water, quickly."

Millie snatched up the glass that had contained the tisane, ran to the galley, and brought it back in a moment filled with fresh, cold water. Anne drank it until the color returned to her face. Then she took a couple of deep breaths.

"Are you telling me … that someone administered monkshood root to my husband and caused a heart attack? Are you both mad?"

"Sadly, no," Georgia said.

"I assume you would not distress me with this outrage to our friendship if you were not certain. What is your proof?"

Georgia did her best to control her emotions and choose her words carefully. "While we were in the kitchen garden earlier, we saw in one corner a small area Millie referred to at the time as a *poison garden*."

Anne covered the barely perceptible swell of her belly with both hands in alarm. "Who would plant such a thing?"

"Some of the plants, I suppose, may have medicinal uses, but our interest quickly centered on the monkshood. One plant had been dug up in its entirety, root and all, from the center of the bed, where its absence would not be remarked."

Anne took a deep breath and let it out slowly. "Are you telling me that Madame Laurent, whose skill at cookery is lauded from here to the Loire, poisoned Gregory?" She sat on the edge of the sofa now, as though she wanted nothing more than to flee.

"No indeed. Anyone on the estate who knew the properties of that plant could have gone into the garden and dug it up," Millie said. "But if you had intended to plant your little lavender back there, the mystery of why she would have chased you away from it so forcefully is solved. Even touching the monkshood will admit the poison to the body."

"Is that the flower garden behind the mulberry, in the corner?"

"Yes," Georgia said. "Just full of poisonous beauty."

Anne sighed and her rigid posture relaxed a little. "I give her credit for trying to keep me safe, though her methods could use some refinement. But what am I to do now?"

"We have, as you said, no real proof of our suspicions other than that disturbed soil in the garden and your dear husband's symptoms matching those described in the book." Millie sat on the other end of the sofa, back straight. "I should like to consult with Doctor Besson to see if he finds these proofs reasonable enough. If he does, then we must apply to the local gendarmerie to find out who could have done this."

"The police?" Anne exclaimed. "Oh, but you mustn't."

"My dear heart, who else?" Georgia asked. "They will investigate, and discover the madman, and they will be made to answer for depriving you and your children of a man so respected and loved."

"But don't you see?" Anne looked from her to Millie in increasing agitation. "The scandal would be dreadful. Newspapers all over the country would have a field day. Gregory only held the title for ten years, but he was so proud of the family and all they had accomplished. Those circular canals, the irrigation systems that extend over nearly all the canton—they are his work. His contribution to the family legacy, which he could only carry out because he was such a skilled engineer. Water was his specialty." She snorted. "He bucked opposition from everyone from the mayor's clerk in Valmy to the editor of *Le Matin* in Paris, to say nothing of his own neighbors. Oh, the arguments he and Stefan Villiers would have over the water—who had the rights to it, where it would go, what it would do, who would have to give up what so that someone else could share the benefits. It went on for most of the time they knew each other."

"And yet he has been so kind," Millie said. "So efficient in a crisis."

"Well, he would be, during a time of mourning. He is a landowner, too, though not on the scale of de Valmy." Anne scrubbed her face with both hands. "Here I am, chasing rabbits to distract myself from the spectre of poison. Who ... *who* would hate Gregory that much? No, it is impossible. I would rather lose my love to a hidden heart condition than believe that."

"But if Doctor Besson should concur it is possible?" Millie asked gently. "Anne, would it not be better for the police to help you? Because—because—" Her throat seemed to close up.

"Dearest." Georgia took Anne's cold hand. "Until just before Gregory's birthday celebration, no one knew you were expecting a child. What if Gregory was killed so that someone else could inherit? And what if, now that everyone in the chateau and all your guests have been informed of your expectations, someone decides to try a second time? What if your baby is in danger—on the chance that it is a boy—and the heir?"

Anne stared at her, her eyes so wide the irises were surrounded by white. "Georgia Brunel," she said on a gasp, "I never knew you could be so cruel."

Tears welled in Georgia's eyes at this terrible rebuke, and dripped down one cheek. She released Anne's hand. But she did not retreat. She could not. "Not cruel, my dearest friend," she choked. "Realistic. We must have the police, as soon as they can be summoned."

"Is there a detachment in Valmy?" Millie asked, clearly trying to stick to facts in order to control her own distress. "I could solicit Doctor Besson's help. He could escort me there and the two of us could make a report."

Anne struggled to control herself. "The closest is in Arles. Miles and miles away. But you will not summon them. I forbid it." She seized Georgia's hand and laid her wet cheek on it. "I am sorry, dear. Please forgive me. This pregnancy has me all at sixes and sevens, snapping at people I love and weeping at all hours. I carried the twins for nine months with less trouble than this one at four."

Georgia turned her hand over to cup her friend's cheek and wipe away her tears with her thumb. "I was just the same with Helena. She would have been a handful had she lived. Perhaps you are carrying a boy who will arrive fighting."

"He may well have to," Anne sighed, giving Georgia's hand a final squeeze and straightening. "My dears, I know you wish to go to the police, but I beg that you will not. Because I have read enough of Sir Arthur myself to know that the first one they will suspect of this terrible crime is the wife. And I do not think the prospect of *la vicomtesse* going into labor in a gaol cell is enough to keep me out of one should they find no proof to the contrary."

Good heavens. This had not occurred to Georgia even once. She struggled to remain positive. "Of course there is no proof. Because you did nothing."

"But someone did. And if what you conjecture is true, they may try again. Tell me, how can one possibly know if monkshood juice is in something one is eating or drinking?"

"The numbness," Millie said slowly, clearly remembering something. "His lordship said at dinner he could not feel his mouth. But what about before that?"

Anne frowned down at her fingers, knotted together in her lap. "No. But he was not the sort to complain. He once returned from a walk up to Edinburgh Castle with a sprained ankle, and didn't even mention it to me."

"The onset of the numbness is fairly quick, I understand," Millie said. "But the sheer number of people who might have done this—and how they might have done it—I am afraid it is all overwhelming."

Georgia did not even want to think of it. She said to Anne, "You loved your husband—you both were looking forward to the baby's birth. You had no reason at all to wish him out of the room, never mind out of your life permanently."

Anne's gaze filled with a pathetic hope that she could be right.

"In any case, with the gendarmerie so far away, it would take them all of a day to come here, and all your guests will be gone by then."

"Why should that make a difference?" Anne asked.

"We have already established that any one of them could have done it," Millie reminded her. "Except the couple from Grenoble. They only came the morning of the funeral."

"Thank goodness for that. Sophie is Gregory's great-aunt and quite the most formidable of the relatives. I should not like to inform her that she is suspected of his death. She would likely drop me down the well for my impertinence."

Georgia tried to tamp down a giggle, but it escaped anyway. "She was magnificent. She gave Sibyl Campbell such a set-down I doubt she will ever recover. I am glad, too, that we do not have to delay her return home."

"Don't forget the cousin from Nice," Millie said. "He came the day before the funeral, and I do not expect he managed to poison anyone before that via tube or by proxy."

"No," Georgia agreed. "We may see them off in good conscience."

A small silence fell as Georgia calculated who among the guests remained.

Anne moved restlessly and rose to walk to the viewing port, where the sun outlined her body with a gentle glow. "Do you really think there is some danger to my baby?"

Georgia considered her next words. Had she ever been forced to say something so difficult? "I think it is dangerous not to consider the possibility."

"But considering it and doing something about it are two

different things. What if we never find out who could have done this heinous thing? If it is a boy, will he have to go through life looking over his shoulder? Will I have to regard every single person in his life with suspicion until both of us are old and grey?"

"I think perhaps the greatest danger is not forty years from now, but as many days," Millie said. "Imagine the poisoner, flushed with success at having got away with it. Would it take much more encouragement to tie up the loose end? For then the Court of Inheritance would be forced to act and the matter decided as it would have been before your announcement."

Appalled silence met these speculations.

An idea popped into Georgia's mind so suddenly she nearly jumped. "Anne, can you still pilot an airship?"

"I don't know." Her friend gazed at her, puzzled. "I suppose it is like riding a velocipede—once you have the knack, you never quite lose it. But you know how the French are. With the way women are discouraged from flying in this present age, you'd think Celeste Blanchard and Loveday Penhale had never touched a balloon, never mind rallied Europe to take on Napoleon in his own skies. Why do you ask?"

"What if you were to take the girls and their governess to visit your parents in Scotland?"

"Georgia, that is brilliant," Millie breathed. "That way, Anne and her baby are out of reach while you and I flush out the guilty party."

"I beg your pardon? You and Georgia?" Anne was clearly so shocked she could hardly form a sentence. "Put yourselves in danger? Certainly not!"

"My dear, did it ever occur to you to wonder how I came by a Zeppelin airship fit for a prince?"

Anne took this swerve in topic in stride. "I assumed your son was extremely generous."

"He is, but *Helena* would strain even a pocketbook belonging to a Dunsmuir. No, she was a gift from the Empress of Prussia. For solving her kidnapping, foiling a plot, and restoring her to her throne."

"What she is saying, not very modestly, is that we have some little experience in matters such as these," Millie said.

"It is not immodest to recount simple facts," Georgia objected.

"Of course not, dear. But perhaps not all at once."

"I see that you two are keeping secrets I cannot ken," Anne said. "But neither can I leave you on your own with a murderer. What kind of hostess would that make me?" She had recovered enough now that her dry humor was returning.

"A prudent and intelligent one," Georgia said, then leaned toward her, serious now. "You must think of your baby. And your daughters. There is a very real risk that if you stay, they will lose their mother as well as their father. We cannot take that risk."

Anne's gaze held hers, and Georgia saw the moment when the decision was made.

"All right. But I shan't take your little imperial gift. Honestly, Georgia, could she not have given you a cuckoo clock?"

"There were extenuating circumstances."

"I'm sure there were. No, I shall take our old faithful *Bonnie Mary*. The crew all live in town and—"

"You cannot bring a crew," Millie said, sitting up in alarm.

"One of them could be connected to the poisoner, and be convinced or coerced into doing harm at second hand. I will teach your governess and the girls what I have recently learned of navigation. Georgia will refresh your memory of engines and vanes, and you will crew her yourselves."

"My girls?" Anne's voice rose slightly in disbelief.

"Every woman should know how to fly to safety," Georgia said with the conviction of experience. "Do not ask me how I learned this incontrovertible fact."

Anne's mouth opened to do exactly that, then closed again. "All right," she said at last. "To own the truth, with the exception of your own bonnie selves, I can think of no one I would find comfort with more than my own parents."

"Excellent." Georgia rose, Millie with her. "We will provision her from our own stores aboard so that no one may slip monkshood or anything else into your galley. Send mademoiselle and the girls up this afternoon for lessons. Pack valises, and in the bustle of Great-Aunt Sophie and Cousin Bernard's departures, I will spirit them aboard."

"In the meantime, eat and drink nothing that someone else has not tasted first," Millie put in. "If you are thirsty, fill the glass yourself. And lock your door when you go to bed."

"Perhaps the girls would like to join us aboard *Helena* overnight?" Georgia said. "We can make a little party of it, to celebrate the completion of their navigation lessons."

Anne shook her head in wonderment. "If I were not convinced before, I certainly am now. The two of you are positively Machiavellian."

"You should have seen us in Venice," Georgia said, grim with the memory. "But I am glad you did not."

CHAPTER EIGHT

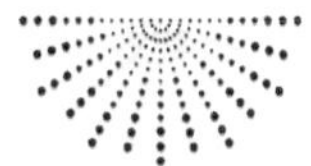

SATURDAY, JUNE 1, AT 1:40 P.M.

My lady,

Thank you for your letter, which alarmed Cornelius and me to the point we nearly pulled up ropes and set our course for Provence. I am very sorry you have lost a friend, and if you do not think it bad manners, I hope you will express my condolences to the widow. I am glad she has you and Miss Brunel there to help her through what will likely be a very trying time.

Marcus is a little older than the vicomte's daughters, but he wants me to say that if he can be of any help in visiting the catacombs or otherwise distracting them from their grief, he is very willing to put himself at their disposal. I suspect he is trying to escape his tutor, but in some cases a father ought to remember it's the thought that counts.

Arrangements for this meeting in Falmouth go on apace. What a tedious business—I have to admire Sir Andrew for his patience. His wife's family pile is near St Michael's Mount, so they are there now. That house—Gwynn Place is its name—is within spitting distance of my uncle's home. He is dead now, as is nearly everyone from that generation, but my grim Aunt Demelza is hanging on by a thread. She was terrifying as a young woman. I can't imagine what she must have been like as a matriarch. I thought they had a couple of daughters, but my father cut off contact with them long before he died, and I was never of a mind to march up to the front door and introduce myself. Likely would have been turned away anyhow.

I wonder if my mind will change once we get down to Falmouth. We lift tomorrow.

I look forward to hearing from you. And to seeing you again. If you are still there by the time our visit to Falmouth is over, we will make good our threats and sail southward. I can hear you now, warning me not to be rude to the earl because I want to be else-where. I'll do my best to obey the voice I cannot forget. Or the lips, either.

Your own
Dustin

Blast and bebother the man! He was not even on the same continent, and yet he could make her blush like a schoolgirl. Georgia folded up the letter and tucked it away in the top drawer of what might have been a bureau had it been free-standing. But the drawers were built into *Helena*'s hull, gently curving as it did. Instead of some prosaic bit of metal to pull them out, each drawer possessed a carved, curved leaf for a pull. To lock the drawers for flight, one simply gave each leaf a quarter turn. Ingenious. She must show Dustin when she saw him again.

But the thought of Dustin in her cabin made the heat

prickle into her cheeks all over again. *Stop it, you silly goose. Go and make some tea.*

They still had no teapot, but following the departure of Anne and the children in an airship of considerable vintage half an hour ago, they would need to lay in a few provisions to make up for those they had shared. A trip into town was becoming more urgent.

But first, she and Millie had to brave the wrath of both the relatives and the staff.

In the drawing room of the chateau, with Millie standing beside her in front of the cold hearth, she gave instructions to both footmen. In twenty minutes, all the guests and staff had assembled, filling the room with whispered speculation.

"Good afternoon," she said in her best Belgravia accents. "For those of you whom I have not yet met, I am Lady Langford, and this is my aunt by marriage, Miss Millicent Brunel. I particularly wish to offer my thanks to you, her ladyship's staff, who have shouldered the burden of the unexpected loss of *le vicomte* with grace and compassion."

Millie translated for those among the staff whose English was not yet fluent.

"And to those of you who were related to *le vicomte*, allow me to again offer our condolences." And her thanks to heaven that two sets of cousins had already departed. She had not been looking forward to informing Great-Aunt Sophie of what she had to tell the people in this room.

"What is the point of this speechifying?" Roger Campbell asked his sister all too audibly.

"The point, sir, is that *la vicomtesse* has asked me to inform you all that she has taken the children to visit their grandparents in Inverness."

"L'Ecosse!" whispered through the staff.

"Inverness!" exclaimed Sibyl. "Why, that's half a hemisphere away."

"Her own mother and father will give her comfort in her and the children's loss, and enable her to resume the reins at Chateau de Valmy in due course." Georgia's tone became businesslike. *"La vicomtesse* has appointed me to run the estate during her brief absence. Let me assure you that you are most welcome to—"

"You!" Roger exclaimed. "What are you to Anne but a friend she hasn't seen in decades? It should be I who runs the estate, as Gregory's nearest relative."

Georgia gazed at him with all the sangfroid of Queen Victoria staring down her Prime Minister, whom she did not like. "Are you accustomed to managing an estate of a thousand acres, with a staff of twenty and guests in residence?"

"No, of course not. But I am, as you will observe, a man. Appointed by God to be the head of the household."

"That may apply to the rooms you share with your sister, sir, but it does not apply to an estate of this size. I have been managing both household and holdings for some years."

"But you—"

"Do you speak French, sir?" Millie inquired, her enunciation declaring how distasteful she found the man.

"No, of course not. Slippery language. Never got the hang of it."

Madame Laurent frowned, the butler's back stiffened in offense, and the footmen translated in a whisper to those nearest.

"I am fluent, as is Lady Langford," Millie said. "I think we have made it abundantly clear that you and your sister are most welcome to stay on, but as honored guests, not as the persons who will give the staff their orders and see to any matters arising in the absence of *la vicomtesse*."

Perhaps she reminded him of his mother, or a governess with whom he'd never got the upper hand. He folded like a deck of cards, muttering angrily to Sibyl, who patted his arm in sympathy. He shook her off and stalked over to the window, where he presented his back to further proceedings.

"Madame Fleury, I regret that your travel plans have been interrupted by these sad events," Georgia resumed. "Please let me know if we can make arrangements for you, or be of service to you in any way."

Manon Fleury thanked her. "I will need a day or two to rearrange my affairs a second time," she said. "But we cannot have you sleeping aboard your airship when there are so many rooms here. I entreat you to return to the rooms *la vicomtesse* gave you." She smiled at Millie. "I know the rose room was a particular delight."

"It was indeed. How kind of you to remember, madame."

Georgia did not need to catch the eye of the housemaids. Madame Chouinard had already tilted her head and they hurried out to prepare the rooms. She did, however, meet the stony gaze of Madame Laurent.

"I beg you will excuse me," the cook said. "I must return to our preparations for dinner."

"Thank you, madame. For that, and for many other things," Georgia said sincerely. "Madame Chouinard, perhaps we might meet in a quarter of an hour to discuss menus?"

"*Oui, madame.*"

"*La vicomtesse*'s lady's maid is here?"

A young woman curtseyed, her masses of black, curling

hair dressed in the new Psyche knot with an elegantly twisted black linen bandeau to match her dress. "I am Valerie Boyle, madame. Do you require my services?"

Boyle? That was not a French name, though her French had the fluency of its being learned at her mother's knee. "I should like very much to discuss them, and to have your advice on a number of matters. Perhaps in an hour?"

"Oui, madame."

Appointments with Monsieur Chouinard the butler and Monsieur Benezet Martin, Gregory's estate manager, followed. Georgia imagined they would rather have dealt with Roger, and bent him to their will without his being aware of it. But she was rather skilled at the art herself, and they would soon know it.

"Thank you all," she said with a gentle inclination of her head. "Among us, we will keep de Valmy running as it should until we can welcome *la vicomtesse* home."

"I should not put myself on a level with the servants in such an endeavor," Sibyl muttered as she and Roger went out. "And her with such airs!"

"Hush, woman," he said in a low tone that Georgia's keen hearing caught without difficulty. "Mind your manners or we'll find ourselves out on our ears looking for cheap rooms in Paris. There are some two weeks yet before the symposium."

It did not take long to go over the menus for the remainder of the week with Madame Chouinard. "And we shall have Monsieur Roger and Mademoiselle Sibyl, as well as Madame Fleury, myself and Mademoiselle Brunel to dinner. Only five," she concluded sadly.

"You might invite Monsieur and Madame Villiers one

evening," the housekeeper suggested hesitantly. "He and *le vicomte* were good friends, despite their many disputes and rages over the water."

"A good suggestion. Shall we say Wednesday?"

Madame nodded, inclined her head, and went out with her sheaf of menus.

Only five. And three of them had very good reasons for wanting poor Gregory out of the way. The geologists would hang on for days, so she could ask them questions at her leisure, but if Manon was making fresh arrangements for her voyage, she must have a tete-a-tete sooner than that.

But first things first: Valerie Boyle, Anne's lady's maid.

The young woman knocked on the drawing-room door frame and Georgia beckoned her in. "Thank you for being so prompt."

"It is important to *la vicomtesse* that her household run in an orderly manner." At Georgia's invitation, she seated herself on the edge of the sofa opposite. "*Merci*, madame, for taking the reins and ensuring that it continues to do so."

"I hope the staff does not think me presumptuous."

"No, indeed. Many of us have heard *la vicomtesse* speak of you with fondness." She shifted and knotted her fingers together. "If you will forgive me, can you tell me whether or not you will require my services?"

Georgia gazed at her. "What are your plans if I do not?"

"If I have no lady to look after, I will go home to Arles, to my mother. My sister lives in Montpelier, my brothers in Marseille. My only living uncle, my late father's brother, is far away—a captain for hire in the Fifteen Colonies. She is not well and it would ease my mind to be close to her awhile."

It made sense, and did the young woman credit. "I expect

your mother will welcome you for two weeks," she said. "Though I would dearly love your services—your hair is a positive triumph—I have become used to doing for myself. *La vicomtesse* estimates her return around mid-month."

Valerie smiled. "I shall be prompt."

When she looked as if she expected a dismissal, Georgia put out a hand. "Just one or two more things, Valerie."

"Of course, madame." She settled on the cushion at attention, her dark brown eyes expectant.

"I wonder if you might tell me what the feelings are downstairs about *le vicomte*'s death."

The young woman's eyebrows rose. "They are desolated, of course—he was a good employer, and did much to improve the tenant farms, especially with irrigation. The old lord was ill for several years, and management of the estates had become burdensome to him. *Le vicomte* let his estate manager go, and brought a classmate from university to take over. Monsieur Benezet Martin was with us earlier."

"Ah." Georgia nodded thoughtfully. "So no one among the staff had quarreled with *le vicomte*, or been offended?"

She shook her head. "The old estate manager was not happy to be—how do the English say? Sacked. But as a man of conscience, he knew that standards had not been kept up. To be fair, with no support from the chateau, his job was made difficult."

"Would he attempt some kind of retribution, do you think?"

"No, never. He found a position quickly. Monsieur Villiers, in fact, was delighted that his services were available. His own estate manager had died in the autumn, in a shooting accident."

That was interesting. Not the poor man's death, but the man who had been sacked going to work for the person who had, according to Madame Chouinard, many "disputes and rages over the water."

"Madame, please do not think me impertinent, but why are you asking me these things?"

Georgia gazed at her. "If you were not going away, I might take you into my confidence, but I will not burden you now."

Alarm flickered in Valerie's eyes. "You believe there has been some mishap? Madame Fleury did everything she could."

Her abrupt reference to the next person on Georgia's mental list surprised her so much it was all she could do to keep her face expressionless. "What do you mean?"

"Why, simply that she employed all the skill she possessed to save him that night. *La vicomtesse* has been gracious enough to allow me to arrange Madame Fleury's hair, and to assist her in dressing in the evenings. She is an interesting person, and believes in education for women, whether that be in the engineering sciences, or medicine, or business."

"I quite liked her before," Georgia said mildly, "but now I admire her. Do you have ambitions along that line?"

"I wish to fly," Valerie said bluntly, after the briefest of hesitations. "I have applied to the flight school at Geneva, but I have been waiting for a place for two years now."

"Because you are a woman?"

Her keen eyes flashed, though whether with anger or with acknowledgement of Georgia's perspicacity, she could not tell. "My uncle Alturas Boyle flies for the Meriwether-Astor Airship Works in the Fifteen Colonies. My cousins, the daughter and son of his and my father's late brother, fly with him, and his wife and children also. When I graduate with my pilot's wings, he has assured me of a place in the company for my father's sake."

"And meanwhile, you exercise your other talents and save your wages."

Valerie nodded.

Some day, Georgia hoped that Teddy would find a woman like this. Not the sheltered, vapid jewel of some Blood family, but a woman of fire and ambition and resilience. "Then allow me to contribute to such a worthy cause," she said on impulse. "I will pay your wages for the two weeks you are with your mother, on the condition that they go toward your nest egg."

Valerie gasped, and she shook her head emphatically. It was a tribute to her skill at hairdressing that the Psyche knot did not come down. "No indeed, madame. I cannot allow it. No one is paid for an absence from their position."

"You will be. Say nothing to anyone. I insist."

Tears pooled in those expressive eyes. "I do not deserve this kindness, madame."

"Oh yes, you do. If it helps to pay your tuition when you are finally accepted, then I am amply rewarded. When do you go to Arles?"

"The train has already departed. Monday, I expect." The wobble of emotion smoothed out of her voice. "Please permit me to dress your hair this evening, madame. It is the least I can do to thank you."

"Done." Georgia held out a hand, and Valerie took it. "And if you show me how to do that lovely style you are wearing, I shall be even more rewarded."

Saturday, June 1, at 3:30 p.m.

MILLIE HAD NOT PLANNED to go to town after their meeting with the guests and staff, but when the butler discovered that the decanter of port he had intended to serve before dinner had mysteriously been drained to the dregs, his outrage knew no bounds.

"I shall not serve that blockhead cousin *le vicomte*'s precious vintages," he fumed to his wife as Millie passed the door of their adjoining offices. "I shall send to the village at once and spend as few francs as possible on a replacement. He may drink that and never know the difference."

"If you behave so outrageously, I will be ashamed of you," Madame Chouinard replied calmly. "But if you do send someone, please have him collect *le vicomte*'s pocket watch. Neither *la vicomtesse* nor that useless valet remembered it was at the horologist's for repair, and it must be collected. It belongs now to his heir."

Millie retraced her steps. "I beg your pardon, but did I hear someone is going into the town? May I go along? Her ladyship has commissioned me to make a number of purchases, and I did not relish the prospect of going in *la vicomtesse*'s farm cart."

Madame Chouinard came close to fainting at the thought of such a spectacle. "My dear madame, you shall do no such thing. The *landau à vapeur* will be waiting at the front steps in half an hour."

Millie had only to fetch a hat from *Helena*, locate her pocketbook, and change into her walking boots, before she was ushered into the family vehicle by the same footman who had served dinner last night. "You are Jean-Pierre, are you not?"

He piloted the vehicle faster than Georgia, but not as fast as Anne. Yet. Millie put a cautious hand to her hat, just in case.

"I am, Madame Brunel."

"Thank you for taking me to the town. I shall do my best not to slow you down."

He laughed and pushed a little on the acceleration bar. Millie held on to her hat in earnest, as the tonneau was not enclosed and the wind screen rather low.

"What do you think of this sad business, Jean-Pierre? Have you been long in service to de Valmy?"

"I came when I was seventeen. I am twenty now. I have not been in service anywhere else, but I cannot imagine a better employer. I am very glad that Monsieur Campbell is not to be the heir. He is not a serious person except on the subject of rocks. No one below stairs likes him, and the sister not much more."

"If *la vicomtesse* does not bear a son, he may yet be the heir, whether any of us likes him or not."

"I am sure *le bon Dieu* would not be so unkind to de Valmy." He paused. "Père Francois would not like me to say it, but it seems He has been plenty unkind to us already."

"The family are fortunate in their priest," she said, glad for the change in topic. "He seems to be just as he ought. Steady, trustworthy."

Jean-Pierre was silent. Millie could see a church steeple beyond the shoulder of a hill. That must signify their destination. "What church is that?"

"Notre Dame d'Esperance, madame. We are nearly there."

"Oh yes, Père Francois told us he was an altar boy there. Someone said he was spoiled, but I could see no evidence of it on the day of the funeral."

With a snort, he blurted, "His father the attorney was forever bailing him out of trouble. He was a few years older than me, but even I knew that if a window was broken or a gate left open between a garden and the pigs, he was probably responsible. Once I heard him say, 'Vengeance is mine, says the Lord, but sometimes the Lord needs a hand.'"

"What do you mean?"

"I mean that if he thought you had raised your hand to him, or spoken out of turn about him, he would make you pay for it." Jean-Pierre, it seemed, could no more hold back his feelings than Millie could let go of her hat. "My older brother's shoulder will never be the same after he was pushed from the haymow."

"What had he done?"

"Kissed a girl who wouldn't give Francois the time of day."

Millie was unwilling to revise her opinions of the young priest so quickly. "Perhaps God has had a chance to reform him," she suggested as the gravel road squeezed between two garden walls and emerged into the town square. Jean-Pierre glided to a halt in front of the church and released a little of the pressure in the boiler.

"That, I believe, is a life's work," the young man said. "Will an hour be sufficient for your errands, madame?"

"Yes, more than sufficient. If it becomes too hot by then, you will find me inside the church."

He helped her descend, and went puttering off, presumably to the horologist.

The little square was charming, with red and purple flowers tumbling from windowboxes, and stone staircases winding up from steep streets on the sloping north side. The square was lined with shops, and bins of fruit and vegetables made a colorful display, as did the windows of the patisserie and fromagerie.

It took all the cheer and bustle of a bright morning to make Millie's spirits rise once more from the depths of her newfound knowledge of Père François. Could that kind, seemingly gentle man really be the vengeful terror Jean-Pierre remembered? And if it were true, how far would he carry his vengeance once stoked to a blaze? Had Gregory Campbell offended the priest and brought such a thing down on his head?

Or was she simply reaching for a quick solution to this terrible tragedy?

For if her speculations were correct, the culprit had to be familiar with the kitchen garden and in particular the poison garden in the corner. And who more familiar than the nephew of the gardener and the cook? He had probably been running wild on the estate since he was a boy.

Millie pushed aside these unhappy thoughts with the help of a china shop on the corner. The first thing her gaze fell upon was a bit of whimsy in the form of a teapot shaped like a hen, presiding over a round tea table laid for two. Her exclamation of delight brought the proprietor out from behind a drape.

"Do you like her, madame?"

"I do, very much." Millie smiled over her shoulder. "I am from England, and we are used to very formal teapots, strictly utilitarian. No one would ever dream of this."

"My daughter makes them." She pointed to the window, where a rosy teapot shaped like a peony in full bloom sat next to a white cat lifting its paw as the spout. "She does not care that people want a simple brown teapot to steep their leaves in. In her opinion, one ought to find joy in one's table arrangements."

"I quite agree with her," Millie said promptly. "Something so small yet so happily made can change one's outlook altogether, and make it easier to face the world. I must have that hen, if you would be so kind."

She added a tin of Provençal lavender tea to her order, and ten minutes later sailed back into the square to risk Madame Laurent's wrath by buying nuts and cheese for private delectation aboard *Helena*.

The apothecary's sign reminded her of her most pressing errand, and after asking for directions to Dr Besson's surgery, found him just escorting a young boy and his mother out the door of the low whitewashed building.

"Stepped in a hornet's nest," he murmured as he ushered her inside, then opened a door to what was clearly his office. "He is fortunate that his older brother was with him. What can I do for you, Madame Brunel?"

Millie set her purchases on the floor next to the chair in front of his desk, and clutched her pocketbook in her lap as she told him what she and Georgia believed. "What we would like to know, doctor, is whether we are making utter fools of ourselves with such wild speculations, or bringing to light a terrible possibility. We resolved to bring these facts to you and solicit your opinion."

A long moment passed in which the doctor's gaze did not move from Millie's face. A hummingbird swooped past the deeply inset window to his left and he did not even blink. He appeared to have been stricken silent. Then, with a breath that told her he had nearly forgotten that lungs needed air, he seemed to come to himself.

"Root of monkshood, dug from the garden."

"Yes. I found the de Valmy children reading a book about wildflowers and asked them to look it up for me. It matches point for point to what we observed that night, and what *la vicomtesse* herself remembers."

"*I cannot feel my face,*" the doctor quoted softly. He got up and considered a section of the bookcases that covered one wall. Selecting a book, he brought it back to his desk. When he found what he was looking for, he read it carefully.

Then he turned the book so that Millie could do the same. But the words blurred into a medical tangle where even her excellent French could not follow. She turned the book back to him. "I cannot understand it as well as I would wish."

He explained in such careful terms that Millie wondered if the authors of the wildflower book had also read it, and reduced it to its most pungent and comprehensible form. "Tell me, madame, what exactly did *la vicomtesse* say about his heart?"

Millie did her best to recollect Anne's words, overlaid as they were now by grief and time. "She said that his heart was galloping as though he'd been running. And then it slowed, and must have given him pain, for he cried out. She tried to find someone to help, but could not, and when she returned, it was beating at a normal speed. Then it slowed once more. Stopped—and that was the end."

He glanced down at the open pages. "It follows." He thought for a moment, then met her gaze again. "It is a unique series of events. Together with the evidence of the root being removed from the ground, and in the absence of any possible explanation to otherwise account for it, I am afraid I concur with the conclusions of you and Lady Langford."

Something coiled tightly in Millie's chest—some remnant of a past in which she had rarely been taken seriously or even heard—loosened and enabled her to breathe. She whispered, "Oh, doctor. I am at once relieved and appalled."

"I am, too," he admitted. "And ashamed I did not understand it sooner. Had I not merely put it down to indigestion—"

"Doctor Besson, you know as well as I that nothing could have saved him. By the time you were called, his condition was already too advanced."

"My mind tells me you are right. But my heart still cannot accept the loss of a good man." He rubbed a hand over his face. "The question we must ask is, what now?"

"*La vicomtesse* forbids us to send for the gendarmes at Arles."

"I do not blame her. The scandal would be immense, and a squadron of strangers marching about the parish would leave us no closer to finding out who did this than if we had ignored it altogether."

The doctor was, Millie could see, somewhat of a cynic, despite pursuing a career based on what could only be called optimism.

"Lady Langford and I are determined to make inquiries," Millie said. "I should like to know that we have you to back us up, whether we are successful or not."

"You realize you run the risk of the same fate—two women poking about where they do not belong. Better I should make these inquiries."

"Perhaps, but Lady Langford is managing the household in *la vicomtesse*'s absence—"

"You convinced her to remove herself and her children from danger?"

"Yes. It was far easier than I thought."

"Perhaps you ought to use the same persuasions on yourself and her ladyship."

But Millie shook her head. "The difficulty and the advantage of being a woman is that people tend to not take us seriously. In this case, we are uniquely placed to exercise our discretion and our intelligence in the service of a friend who needs both. Forgive me, doctor, but we will not be turned aside."

"I suspected as much." He smiled, and with it the lines of care were erased from his face and one could almost forget the hair turning white at temples and forehead. "I have never met anyone like the two of you. Madame, would it be impertinent of me if I asked you to set aside these grim possibilities and allow me to take you to dinner some evening?"

A blush cascaded through Millie's person from head to foot. But there was only one answer she could give, considering the precious letter that even now lay concealed in her pocketbook. "I very much appreciate your offer, doctor. But my heart has made its choice of another, and I must be faithful to it."

With a sigh, he nodded. "Then I will remain your staunch friend, and you may call for my assistance at any time, day or night."

She rose and offered him her hand, and instead of gripping it in a handshake, he lifted it to his lips and kissed it. The surprise carried her all the way across the square to where Jean-Pierre waited.

CHAPTER NINE

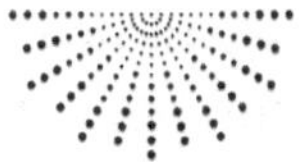

5:10 P.M.

Georgia was in her cabin aboard *Helena*, trying to decide whether she should move her traveling closet into the house for convenience or stay on the airship for safety.

Helena curtsied with the weight of someone setting foot on the gangway, and in a moment, Georgia could hear Millie's voice. "Yes, I know this is all strange and new to you. But believe me, you are much better off. Just leave them there by the table, Jean-Pierre, thank you."

Something cried out, and Georgia abandoned her cabin forthwith. "Millie? Is everything all right?"

"It is now," came her aunt's voice, a little grim around the edges. "I apologize for not seeking your approval first, but prompt action was warranted."

Millie stood in the dining saloon, removing her gloves. A parcel the size of a breadbox lay on the table, along with a book nearly as large. A covered basket sat on the floor at her feet, and another mournful cry came from within.

"I had to take them," she said, in a tone as close to defiant as Georgia had ever heard it. "He was about to slaughter them, because they would not lay, when they are half starved and abused and cannot muster a cluck, never mind an egg."

"What are?" Georgia knelt to release the catch, and cautiously lifted the lid.

Two miserable hens gazed up at her. On meeting her eyes, one of them flinched and hid beneath the tail of the other. Patches of pebbled skin fore and aft looked pink and angry, the shafts of feathers lay exposed to view, and the comb of the first looked as though it had been cut at some point in the past. Both of them were filthy with mud and excrement.

"Oh, Millie," Georgia said on a sigh of pity. "I would have done the same."

"I am glad to hear it. He is a beast, that man, but he is well compensated. The first order of business is a bath. While I do that, we shall exchange our news of the afternoon. I bought a teapot, too. And Doctor Besson directed me to a bookshop."

Georgia thought perhaps a discussion of poultry hygiene might wait until Millie's crusading spirit had calmed a little. While she ministered to the hens, who did not so much as squawk at being immersed in warm, soapy water, Georgia unwrapped the teapot.

She laughed in delight. "Millie, it's perfect. I shall make tea this minute and we will have it outside."

"I thought the same. Come, my dears. You shall have some grass and some sunshine."

In a few minutes, she and Millie had spread a wool blanket on the grass beneath *Helena*'s bow, poured tea into the cups with their Zeppelin crest, and watched the wet hens cautiously exploring their new surroundings.

"I suspect your trip to town was more informative than

my conversations with the staff," Georgia said, sipping the rather lovely lavender-scented tea Millie had brought. "I spoke with Valerie Boyle, Anne's lady's maid, and was fascinated to discover that in addition to her skills with hair and dress, she wants to be a pilot. The flight school at Geneva has been keeping her waiting for two years. Presumably while male candidates are accepted ahead of her."

"A woman of parts." Millie kept a close eye on the hens, who did not seem inclined to wander. One of them yanked a worm out of the ground and they divided it between them. "I cannot tell what breed these two are supposed to be, but they are speckled in the front and solid at the tail."

"I suspect we will have a better idea when they recover their feathers."

"Did Miss Boyle shed any light on *le vicomte*'s death?"

"No, only reiterated how much he was respected and missed. The estate agent, a Monsieur Benezet Martin, was a little more forthcoming. He is a blasted tree of a man who speaks English as fluently as you speak French."

"Blasted? Is he infirm of body?"

"A limp, and a withered hand, the result of some childhood disease, which he made no bones about telling me. But his intelligence is fearsome, and from what I saw, he is heard only to be obeyed. Even Monsieur Laurent takes his orders without complaint. I gather he is deeply respected for bringing all three of the de Valmy estates back to their former glory—not without some kicking and screaming, but back nonetheless."

"What is his opinion, then?" Millie asked. "I take it we need not suspect him, if he was a longtime friend of *le vicomte*?"

Georgia smiled around another sip of tea. Really, it and the sunshine and clean hens were a tonic to the soul.

"We need not suspect him. In fact, he had a list ready for me—several people I had not thought to suspect, including *la vicomtesse* herself, the priest, the doctor, and most of all, Stefan Villiers."

Millie set her cup into its saucer with a *clink*. "Jean-Pierre will agree with him about the priest. Apparently he was quite a hellion, unable to bear slights or mistreatment and punishing those who offended him. Did Monsieur Martin know Père François in his youth?"

"No, he has only been here eight years. I confess I find it difficult to believe such things of that gentle young man, but here are two accounts of him that match."

Millie picked up her cup once more. "Did he survive accusing your friend Anne of poisoning her husband?"

"Anne herself told us she would be the first person suspected." Georgia's gaze returned to Millie from the hens, who were snipping off bits of grass and eating them. "Apparently she and Gregory had a dreadful quarrel two nights before he died. And that same morning, she quarrelled with Madame Laurent. Monsieur Martin had the temerity to call my friend a *dockside harpy,* since the latter argument could be heard right through the stone walls."

Millie choked on her tea, and Georgia patted her back until she recovered. "Did you sack him?"

"I couldn't. I have had many a quarrel with Anne since we met at school, and only wish I had thought of *dockside harpy* myself."

"Georgia! That does not make her guilty. She was devastated at Gregory's death. And you know she loved him deeply."

"I do. But now we have sent her away, and outside of pursuing her to Inverness to ask her the nature of their quarrel, I do not know what to do. What did you learn besides where to purchase an enormous book?"

"It is the same one as in the library here, with an extensive description of the effects of monkshood, among its many other entries. I thought I had better get it, in case we run into other cases of poisoning." Millie gave a sigh. "I do wish we could manage a simple holiday just once."

"Says the woman who braved a man with a cleaver in his hand to save a couple of bedraggled birds."

"It was a knife. There are things I will leave out of my correspondence with Cornelius, that's certain," Millie admitted. "I will tell him about the hens to delight Marcus, and leave out the details. In the meanwhile, what is our next course of action?"

"I suppose I must send a pigeon to *Bonnie Mary* and ask Anne the nature of the quarrel with her husband. Though how I am to do that without offending her is something I must think through very carefully."

"But if their quarrel followed on the first, with Madame Laurent, I wonder if the two events might have been connected. Madame told Anne something, and then she went straight to Gregory to have it out with him."

But Georgia was already shaking her head. "I cannot nemagine anything a cook would have to say to a viscountess that would make her turn and quarrel with her husband. That she proposed to make something he didn't like for dinner?" Millie tilted her head in rueful acknowledgement. "I cannot think of any subject that would connect two arguments between employer and employed. Monsieur Martin seemed to think it quite serious. Anne did not come down to dinner, but took a tray in her room."

"You might confirm that with Miss Boyle, who might have been privy to a detail or two," Millie suggested. "But Georgia, consider what Anne herself said—that she was snapping at people she loved and weeping for no reason. Could it not simply have been the pregnancy affecting her, and the disagreement was about something quite benign?"

"I suppose it could," Georgia admitted. "I will speak to Miss Boyle. What do you think we ought to do about Père Francois?"

"If he has a talent for vengeance, I am not inclined to do anything," Millie said with emphasis. "What reason could he have to harm his patron?"

"Vengeance?"

"Very amusing, dear. But in response to what? That young man is either the best actor we've ever seen—Drury Lane included—or he truly admired and respected de Valmy. The latter seemed to permeate every moment of that funeral service."

"Perhaps I will invite him to tea, and ask if their relationship was as good as it appeared to be. And if I am not satisfied, I may go to Monsieur Laurent, his uncle, and ask him the same."

Millie shook her head. "You speak to the priest, and I will speak to the gardener. He is more likely to tell me the truth than a titled woman with the power to turn him out of his position."

"I am not likely to risk the displeasure of his wife and her cleaver."

"Still."

Millie was right. Georgia, watching the hens hunt, asked, "Have you given any thought to the accommodations of our feathery guests?"

Millie nibbled her lower lip. "I confess I hadn't progressed much past getting them aboard. Marcus's adopted hens seem to have slept in *Foresight*'s piping, and he was forever trotting after them with a rag."

"Not the most appealing thought," Georgia said. "I suppose the basket will have to do until we find something more suitable. You are determined they shall travel with us?"

"With your permission." Millie turned a pleading gaze upon her. "I hope you will give it. I have never had a pet, though Teddy was kind enough to share all of his menagerie with me."

Georgia could not bear the thought of a single moment of disappointment ever again entering Millie's life, and certainly not at her hands. "Dearest, this vessel belongs to us equally. If you wish to crew it with hens, then that is what we will do. In the meanwhile, you might consult with the poultry keeper here on how to bring them back to health, and what is the best means of feeding and housing them."

With every word, the humility faded and joy filled Millie's eyes. "I shall begin teaching them manners. Luckily, they seem to have lost their fear of us."

As she spoke, the braver bird ventured on to the blanket to inspect the teapot. When Millie offered her some of the cheese, she took it so politely that Georgia was astonished.

The more fearful one could not be convinced to approach, but snapped up the cheese when it was gently tossed.

"Come, ladies," Millie said, rising to her feet and collecting both teapot and cheese. "If you follow me aboard, you may have more."

The hens did not need to be asked twice. Georgia brought up the rear, bearing empty teacups and fresh questions. For how could there be so many people in conflict with Gregory —enough to wish him such a painful death?

Saturday, June 1, 1895
Chateau de Valmy

Dearest Anne,

Be assured all is well here, and our inquiries are proceeding even as you sail northward. I expect by now the girls have just waved to the bell ringers at Rouen Cathedral. I urge caution, however, in passing over St Malo. It has, I understand, a reputation as a pirate haven.

A tidbit of information came to our attention this afternoon. Apparently you had words with Madame Laurent a few days before Gregory's death? And about the same time, raised voices were heard between you and he? Forgive me, dearest, but if we are to ferret out a poisoner, we must close every door until he has no escape. Can you tell me the nature of both contretemps? And consequently why you might have taken a tray in your room at the end of it all?

I would be grateful for your confidence.

In other news, my aunt conferred with Dr Besson, who consulted a fearsome tome of a botanical nature. Both he and it concluded that our speculations are grounded in fact. He concurs with us that monkshood root was the means. Now we have only to discover motive and opportunity.

I should very much like to know how the juice of the monkshood root was administered. Can you think of an occasion, no matter how trivial, when it might have been added to Gregory's food or drink before we all met on the terrace that last evening? Because I remember thinking he was not well as we were conversing before dinner, and when he took me in to the dining room, he was trembling. The poison, I conclude, was already doing its dreadful work.

Goodness, I wish I had been able to ask you these things during the past week! But we were not certain, and now that we are, I must use what I have—paper and pigeons.

Let me know soonest. I embrace you and the girls.

Your faithful friend,

Georgia

Georgia folded the thin stationery commonly used for mail between non-fixed addresses, admired the Zeppelin crest on the brass body of her very own pigeon as she tucked the letter inside, and rolled the numbers and letters on its bow to form the code for *Bonnie Mary*. Its engine ignited and with a lift of its brass pinions, it swooped into the chute and in seconds was beyond all human reach.

Sunday, June 2, after church and lunch

Georgia found Valerie Boyle in Anne's dressing room, apparently setting everything to rights for *la vicomtesse*'s eventual return, though it was the Lord's day and a half day off for the staff.

"Madame." Valerie curtseyed. "As you see, I am leaving everything ready before my departure tomorrow."

Georgia smiled and waved her into Anne's bedroom, where the window seat beckoned as a comfortable place in which to share confidences. After a moment's hesitation, Valerie seated herself on the far side, once again on the edge of the square cushion.

Perhaps it was best to ease into the subject gradually. "You have your ticket and your bag packed?"

The young woman nodded. "I shall travel on the seven o'clock milk train tomorrow morning, and will return on the fourteenth. My mother is overjoyed. Thank you, madame, for enabling me to make her so happy."

While Georgia's relationship with her own mother before her death had not been so cordial, she was able to appreciate relatives who loved and were loved in return. "I am glad. I am also interested in your plans for the future, as I am sure your mother is as well. If one is not admitted to flight school, are they then doomed to stay on the ground? For it is not like this in England. One practices with an experienced pilot, learns all they can, and then takes the examinations. Only if one wishes to join the Royal Aeronautic Corps does a candidate receive specialized training. Flying for the Corps in defense of the country is not like taking a personal vessel to a distant friend's for tea."

Valerie shook her head. "It is the opposite here. One learns to fly at an accredited school, which includes military training —even simulated battles. Cadets take the examinations, and if they pass, only then can they set a hand to the helm of a ship not dedicated to training, whether a personal or a military vessel." She smiled, a dimple denting her cheek. "But if, say, one's late father were a pilot and instructed a young person for several months with no one the wiser, then all a cadet can do is try not to show they know too much during classes."

"I think that might be difficult for you, *non?*" Georgia asked with a return smile.

"It would be a price I was willing to pay," she said with a sigh. Then her gaze flicked up. "But I am sure you did not seek me out to talk of flight school."

"I do appreciate the information, however. Now I am hoping you may have additional information on a different subject." Valerie waited expectantly. "I understand that a few days before *le vicomte's* death, her ladyship spoke with Madame Laurent in heated terms. Do you happen to know what they could have been quarreling about?"

"*Non, madame. La vicomtesse* could sometimes be short-tempered, but I never heard her lose her temper with Madame Laurent. Very few in the chateau would. One does not wish to offend a woman who has only to lift a hand to receive fifty offers of employment from other noble families."

"I see." Perhaps Valerie had not witnessed Anne's behavior, then. But it still could have happened. "And what about later? I understand that she and de Valmy quarrelled, upsetting *la vicomtesse* to the point that she took a tray in her room that evening. You must have seen her then. Spoken, perhaps? Received a confidence?"

Valerie's long lashes fell on her dusky cheeks, where a flush burned along her cheekbones. "I would not betray my lady's confidence, even if I had."

"Nor should you. But I have just now written to Anne to ask the same questions. You see how useful it will be if one can corroborate the other."

Clearly it had not yet occurred to the girl that anything her lady said might need to be corroborated. "*La vicomtesse* was upset that she had quarrelled with her husband, whom she adored."

"And do you know the nature of this quarrel?" Georgia held her breath.

"She did not take me so far into her confidence, madame."

Georgia let out the breath on a disappointed sigh.

"But I do know her appetite was poor. She hardly touched the tray. And when I encouraged her to at least take a little soup, she said something very strange."

Georgia waited, hope springing eternal.

"She said that too much knowledge lent as unpleasant a flavor to food as too much salt."

Turning this over in her mind, Georgia could find no way to understand its meaning. "Did she elaborate?"

"No, madame. She simply pushed away the tray and said she wished to rest. The pregnancy, you know."

"Yes, of course. She said it was making her both snappish and weepy, poor darling."

"It was indeed. When I offered to go with her to *l'Ecosse* yesterday, she did snap at me. I tried not to be offended. It was only the pregnancy talking," Valerie concluded sadly.

Georgia squeezed her hand and rose. "Do not take it to heart. Thank you for your honesty."

"I regret I could not be more helpful, madame. If I remember anything else, I will come find you."

"*Merci*. Do you happen to know if Père François is still in the chapel?"

"He departed after our service here. He is saying another mass."

"Oh?" Another one? But then, she was a stranger to the community and its customs.

"Yes, for a baby boy, very much wanted. The family often request more than one for the repose of the innocent soul. It was terribly sad—apparently the labor was so difficult he did not even draw breath."

A cold pang of memory whispered through Georgia's body. She had been injured and distraught over Helena's death following a difficult birth, and had not been able to attend her funeral. Even after more than a decade, the grief had not left her.

As for the priest, she would leave him to his duty and pursue another course.

CHAPTER TEN

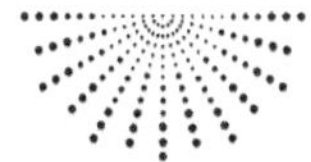

SUNDAY, JUNE 2, AT 2:25 P.M.

She found Manon Fleury in the morning room, arranging a bouquet of roses, freesia, and the inevitable lavender. The woman looked up as Georgia came in, and snipped a stem of a peach-colored rose that somehow exactly matched the stripe in the upholstery of the chair in front of the escritoire. Then she slipped it into place.

"Madame," she said pleasantly. "I hope you are not finding the afternoon too warm?"

"I do not think an afternoon can be too warm for me," Georgia said, just as pleasantly. "In England, you know, the temperature rarely reaches the heights you enjoy here. Provence is where many of my countrymen come for the winter."

"*Oui*, there is quite an enclave of the English in Nice and Cap d'Antibes, I understand. But they keep mainly to themselves."

Georgia had never had much patience with small talk. "I see you enjoy flowers as much as my aunt does." When

Manon smiled, she went on, "Did you study botany at the university?"

"Botany, and biology, and physics. Chemistry. The usual sciences when one intends to be a doctor."

"It must have been difficult to leave, having put in all that work."

"Ah, but the advantage of study is that one can bring it along." She tapped her temple with a spray of lavender before tucking it into the bouquet. "I have not regretted it. My husband and family have made sure my skills were exercised on their various bumps and bruises, rhumes and fevers."

"Your family—including *le vicomte*." Georgia shook her head. "Such a terrible night." Manon regarded the bouquet with great attention, but Georgia had the feeling she did not really see it. "May I ask a somewhat personal question?"

Manon looked up, and for the first time Georgia noticed that her eyes were a similar azure color to those of Gregory. A little more green, perhaps, but still rather arresting when contrasted with her dark hair and sunkissed skin. "But of course."

"That night—after midnight. When you had done all you could for *le vicomte*, and the doctor had gone home for a few hours' rest. *La vicomtesse's* cry for help woke me, but when I went to find you, you were not in your room. Would you mind telling me where you had gone?"

It was too much to hope that Manon would confess to running downstairs to hide the evidence of concocting a poison draught. But her absence in the midst of catastrophe had been bothering Georgia for days, and if she did not ask, she would soon have no opportunity. At some point, the woman had to join her husband and children in Nantes, did she not?

"I often wake in the night," Manon said. "To fetch a glass of water, to visit the water closet. I expect it is the result of having three children so close together. One learns to sleep lightly."

"You were in the water closet?" Oh goodness. What a fool she must look, seeing evil in the most banal of nocturnal errands.

"I was exhausted, but having difficulty falling asleep. I decided to go for a walk."

"A walk? Outside?"

"No, on the roof."

She must have misunderstood her French. "I beg your pardon? Did you say on the *roof*?"

Manon smiled, and two little seedlike dimples appeared mischievously at the corners of her mouth. "One cannot walk in the gardens in one's nightclothes, for fear of the watchman. And pacing the gallery's creaky floors would disturb everyone. As a child, during visits here, I fell into the habit of exploring the roofs. My sisters and I would play up there during the day, and nights with a full moon were almost like daylight."

Georgia was silent with astonishment.

"Would you like to see?"

A blunt refusal hovered on Georgia's lips. Then she forced it back. She might learn something. "Thank you. I never dreamed of having an experienced guide on such an adventure."

Manon tidied up the dropped petals and cut stems and threw them into the fireplace. Then she set the beautiful arrangement in its porcelain vase on the escritoire. "*La vicomtesse* often likes the roses so."

"Then we will keep up her traditions until her return."

Manon led her upstairs—up again to the nursery and the staff rooms. Then she opened a narrow oak door that must surely have been cut from the original forest five hundred years ago. Weathered iron hinges did not screech, evidently as well maintained as those in the family apartments. Beyond was a set of stairs so steep they were almost a ladder. "Are you able for this, madame?"

Georgia would not be offended. "I am only thirty-eight. Not so many years older than you. But if I struggle, you have my permission to haul me up like a bag of flour."

Manon's eyes twinkled. "I will remind you of that if the time comes."

Georgia threw her skirts over one arm and followed her guide up to the attics. An arched doorway in the stone decanted them onto a long walkway on the house's ridgeline, shaded on the near end by the soaring vault of the chapel and on the other by what had once been guard towers on either side of the bridge. The roof was of bluish-grey slate, the dormers and towers of pale Provençal stone, and despite the strong breeze, the sun was hot.

"I should be terrified to come up here at night," she confessed, following Manon cautiously along the walkway. It was only two feet wide, and the roof fell away on either side so steeply that there would be no saving oneself. Even the protruding gables spaced along its considerable length would do nothing to stop anyone so unfortunate as to lose their balance.

"When one is a child, one has no fear. And when it

becomes a refuge, there is more to appreciate than to avoid." Manon paused about halfway along. "From here, one can see the castle gardens, the lake, and much of the irrigation works of which *le vicomte* was so proud."

So one could. Their approach in the airship had given Georgia a good idea of the estate's vastness, but even the gardens extended a good quarter mile in each direction from the banks of the lake. In the distance, she could see the steam-powered machines that must pump the water through the canals, nodding and bowing to each other as they worked.

"Can we see the kitchen gardens from here?" she asked casually. "We are not permitted to enter, but surely one may look from a respectful distance." She would keep rather a respectful distance from the other woman, if it came down to it. Not that she thought Manon was a murderer, exactly. But until she was proved innocent, it was prudent to stay out of arm's reach.

"Of course." Her guide pointed. "I will show you my special spot."

An ancient hexagonal tower intersected the roof line at the three-quarter mark, where the house's wings extended to either side like the cross shape of a church. Inside was an empty stone room with six unglazed arches spaced around it. Pigeons took flight from the sills and soared away over the lake. In the ribs of the vault overhead, a swallow peered down, the cheeping of her fledglings silenced at this unexpected danger.

"See?" Manon waved her to the window. "I can see Monsieur Laurent transplanting something. A lemon tree, perhaps."

So he was. And there were the knot gardens of herbs, and

the neat spirals of those used most—chives, basil, cilantro. Long rows of different varieties of lettuces alternated with the darker green of spinach and chard, beans and peas.

"I do appreciate beauty as well as usefulness," she remarked.

The sill of the embrasure was quite low. It would only take a little leverage on Manon's part to put her off balance, and her own weight would do the rest. It was a sheer drop straight into the lake. Georgia stepped away and strolled to the next opening.

"Does Madame Laurent grow flowers back there in the corner?" She pointed. "They seem rather informal and disarrayed, don't they? A contrast to the wonderful order of the rest."

"I do not know. It was not there when we were children, and a different cook worked here. It was she who planted the knot gardens, but under the old lord, everything was run down. It is a credit to the Laurents that it is so useful now. I suppose madame is entitled to her flower garden, if she wants it."

"Have you been there to cut flowers for the bouquets?"

Manon laughed. "No indeed. Madame would not countenance even the request for permission, never mind my clumsy feet in her garden. Did you know she chased out *la vicomtesse* one day, who only wanted to plant a bit of lavender?"

"She told us," Georgia said with an answering smile. "So you, who have looked down upon every slate of the chateau's roof, have never been in the kitchen garden?"

Manon shook her head. "Not since I was a child. Now, I would not dare. One does not defy Madame Laurent." After a moment, she said, "Now that you know the way to my special place, you may share its peace with me. I shall not chase you out with a cleaver."

Laughing, Georgia swept her a curtsey. "You may enjoy its peace in splendid solitude. I would not have the courage to come up here without you."

"Then we will do so on another visit. I am expecting a tube at any time, confirming my seat on the train to Nantes tomorrow. My husband and mother-in-law assure me that our tickets on the van Meere line are transferable. We expect to sail on Thursday."

Georgia had acted just in time. The risk of taking a tumble down the roof of the chateau had been a price worth paying.

"I am glad you will have happier prospects to look forward to," she said sincerely as she went down the narrow stair facing inward, her skirts once more over her arm. "I will miss your company at the table, I must say."

"You are a woman of resources," Manon assured her on the next steep flight. She closed the old door carefully and turned the key. "You will survive your meals with the Campbells with grace, I am certain."

Georgia was proud of herself for not grimacing in the unladylike fashion this remark deserved.

Monday, June 3 at 9:15 a.m.

After determining that no pigeon from Anne had arrived in *Helena's* communications cage during the night, Millie accompanied Georgia down to the chateau and thence to the breakfast room, hoping that they might have it to themselves.

Manon Fleury had departed on an early westbound train, so their numbers were down by one. But all hope was dashed as they entered to find Sibyl and Roger Campbell already at the hot buffet, dishing up as though none of the other guests currently in the house ever planned to do the same.

"Good morning," Georgia said cheerfully, joining them with her plate.

Millie, a little farther back, distinctly saw Roger slide a chop back into the cream sauce and onions with a guilty look. He already had two on his plate, for goodness sake. She helped herself to a chop—not that one—and added a piping hot boiled egg, some fresh tomatoes and olives, and one of the croissants that needed no butter, they melted so delightfully upon the tongue. Georgia preferred a cold filet of a delicate white fish, likely caught that morning, with her egg, and slices of canteloupe with strawberries.

"Are you planning to explore for more fossils today?" Millie asked pleasantly as she seated herself opposite Sibyl. "It might be wise to go early, if it means to be as warm as yesterday."

"Do we have permission to do so?" Roger asked around a mouthful of his chop.

"Permission from whom?" Georgia cut a strawberry, then speared a bit of melon and ate them together.

"Why, from you," he said. "Since you are in charge here now."

She gazed at him. "There is no need to be snide, Mr Campbell. I have no authority over your movements. You are a welcome guest at Valmy and may do as you please." She checked herself. "Except enter the kitchen garden. Apparently none of us is welcome there, even Anne."

Sibyl sniffed. "What cheek."

"Do you have a penchant for knot gardens, Miss Campbell?" Millie asked with a smile. "I confess I do. Imagine my disappointment when I learned I could not ramble about Madame Laurent's domain. I shall have to make do with Langford Park, I suppose, though its old gardens are more a memory than a reality at the moment."

"If you ask me, Miss Brunel, you ought to put that woman in her place and do as you like," Roger said. "Can't imagine any servant bossing her betters in England."

"Ah, but then I would likely have to cook my own meals. Or choke down what I was given, no matter how unappetizing. The punishment would far exceed the crime, I am afraid. I have not the courage for it."

"Hmph," he said around half an egg. Millie looked away.

"In answer to your question," Sibyl said, "I do enjoy knot gardens. So English."

"What do you like best about them?" Millie was honestly interested. As long as they were not discussing rocks, she was happy to make conversation.

"The order. The containment of plants that would grow madly everywhere, with no discipline, if it were not for careful cultivation."

"Some plants are meant to grow madly, though, don't you think?" Georgia savored her fish. "The wildflowers in the meadows going down to the cliffs, for instance. What a shame it would be to contain them when their beauty is in their lack of discipline."

"I am speaking of vegetables and herbs, your ladyship," came the reply. "Things that must be contained so that they may be harvested. Those lawns outside should be mowed, and soon. I found ladybugs on my skirts yesterday, and I know they came from walking."

A woman who described herself as a naturalist, and she objected to ladybugs? "I am sure Monsieur Laurent will have that well in hand after they have gone to seed," Millie put in before Georgia could say what was clearly on the tip of her tongue. "Do you grow flowers at home in England?"

"We live in a terrace in Lyme Regis," Roger said stiffly. "Not much room to waste on flowers. Excellent location for specimens, however. They rather fill the garden."

"If I must cut flowers, the elderly lady next door allows me to bring over my scissors," Sibyl said. She appeared to be thawing out. Millie only needed to bide her time.

"What are your favorites?"

"I saw a garden in Normandy last year that was all in white," Sibyl said, her usual brusque tone softening. "Several varieties of narcissus, tulips, and even roses just coming out."

"How lovely," Georgia said. "Almost bridal."

Sibyl addressed her chop with some vigor. "One may enjoy a garden without being reminded of matrimony."

Millie said hastily, "I confess my favorites are the blue ones. Perhaps it is because unclouded skies lift my spirits. Delphiniums, bluebells, lilac, hydrangea ... even the bachelor buttons outside in the meadow. They seem so cheeky, don't they, in their enjoyment of their freedom?"

"That cook has delphiniums in her garden, if you like blue," Roger said, clearly considering this a great concession to civility.

"Now, Roger, I've told you before—those are hollyhocks," his sister chided. "Delphiniums are much more delicate."

"Has she indeed?" Millie tried to look pleased. "She has flowers in the kitchen garden?"

"Half wild, they are," Sibyl said. "I had a look through the window when I went down to get some pumice to clean a fossil. She must expend all her discipline on the vegetables, leaving none for flowers. Such a silly differentiation. It shows weakness."

Millie bit her lip to keep from bringing up the ladybugs.

"I could have sworn those were foxglove." Georgia sounded puzzled. "The flowers look like little trumpets, do they not?"

"Not in the least," Sibyl told her. "They are delphiniums. I will swear by it."

"You will not need to swear," Millie said helpfully. "I have a book that has lovely painted plates of hundreds of flowers. We could identify the ones you speak of."

"Can't get close enough for a good comparison." Roger huffed. "We are being prevented from pursuing scientific inquiry by the upstart pretensions of a *cook*. How did my late cousin put up with it?"

"Ah, well," Millie said, rising to investigate the buffet, and in particular the bowl of fresh raspberries with an accompanying lime drizzle. "At least you know where the fossils are. I should like to find an ammonite. Such an appealing shape."

"Their shape is the least of their many attractions, Miss Brunel." Such a change as came over the man now that he was standing on more familiar ground. "We have seen signs of ammonites on the beach below. Perhaps we might tempt you to join us on a little expedition this morning. I should be happy to help you find a suitable specimen to take home."

"Only one, Mr Campbell," she cautioned him. "We must be careful not to exceed *Helena*'s weight limits."

For some reason he found this funny, and unbent long enough to help himself to the third chop.

"YOU CAN'T MEAN to go down the cliffs with those two," Georgia said in a low tone as they walked back to *Helena*. Millie needed to change into walking boots. "It's clear they don't know monkshood from a—a monk."

"They could be playing us for fools," Millie said. "A scientist simply cannot be so unobservant that he cannot tell a delphinium from a hollyhock—or from monkshood, come to that. Something so lethal must be identified with more than *tall* and *blue* as its criteria."

"I rather think that their field of study is not only narrow, but its walls are high enough to keep all other knowledge at bay."

"You may be right. But Georgia, are you really convinced of Madame Fleury's innocence?"

"I am, truly. First, she did all she could in Doctor Besson's presence."

"Well, one would, wouldn't one? But later, when she could not be found—I still find it hard to believe what you told me last night. On the roof? At two in the morning?"

"Apparently so. She finds it comforting. I found it terrifying—and that was in broad daylight."

"It is also impossible to verify."

Georgia was silent. Then she said, "Oddly, I believe her. And I believe also that she was telling the truth when she said she had not been in the kitchen garden since she was a child.

She was quite sincere, and you know, we have seen no evidence of lies or half-truths or even so much as a fib in conversation with her."

Millie had to acknowledge that this was so. "And that night … she was on the terrace as we arrived, with the other guests. I suppose she had no opportunity to slip a lethal poison into *le vicomte*'s wine."

"She does not seem so underhanded."

Millie returned to the matter at hand. "And if the Campbells are really so inexpert with plants that they could not identify the poisonous one they needed on sight, then who is left?"

"Stefan Villiers," Georgia said. "The neighbor known to have quarreled regularly with Gregory over the irrigation systems. And his new estate agent. I still want to speak to them both. I shall send an invitation to dine with us on Wednesday."

Millie conceded that Stefan was indeed suspicious. She would leave him to Georgia. "I know I said I would speak to Monsieur Laurent. But I feel I should close the door for certain on the Campbells. Hence my willingness to risk life and limb on those cliffs." She changed her footwear and regarded her faithful old boots with satisfaction. They would see her down to the beach and back again. "Now I must find a hat. And gloves. For I have no doubt I shall be made to dig up my own specimen as a form of scientific discipline."

"Better you than I," Georgia said, most unhelpfully. "I saw Monsieur Laurent outside the garden walls just now. Perhaps I will ask him for some honey to take with us."

"We have two weeks yet, dear, before we may think of leaving," Millie pointed out.

"But the murderer may not. Even now he may be watching us. Listening behind doors to what we say. We must be careful not to discuss any of this outside *Helena's* lovely hull—and even then, stay away from the viewing ports."

A morning spent with the geologists in the sea air did not sound so bad after all.

CHAPTER ELEVEN

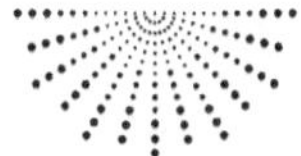

10:40 A.M.

$\mathcal{M}$onsieur Laurent, sadly, was no longer where Georgia had last seen him, placidly trimming back the ivy growing in green abandon on the garden walls. The ground was littered with trimmings, but she was not about to hike the length and breadth of the home acres in search of the compost heap. She would just have to send for him later.

She reconstructed the bird's eye view of the chateau's surroundings in her mind—kitchen garden, formal gardens, lake, orchards, stables, carriage house. Its home acres were larger than those of Langford Park, and the surrounding estate could have housed two of the Park, she was quite sure. How, in all these acres, was one to find a poisoner? And how on earth had the poison been administered? If they could only discern *that*, they might have asked people where they had been.

Think, Georgia. Think about who was on the terrace that evening.

But her memory was like a kaleidoscope, moving and

turning, people coming and going. People she hadn't known then, so faces were a blur without the settling effect of a closer acquaintance. The priest, for one. Manon had stood out eventually, with her striking looks and ability. And Stefan Villiers had differentiated himself not only by his patrician nose and brow, but also by not being related to anyone present.

And really, who went down to dinner expecting one's host to be murdered within the hour? Well, the poisoner, obviously. Someone who had mingled, perhaps, conversing and laughing and casually slipping a vial of lethal juice into Gregory's wine? One would have to conceal such a thing. In a waistcoat pocket? That would point to a man. In one's bodice? A woman would have to be very careful that no drop touched the skin, if it could be absorbed into the body as the doctor had said.

But what if that were not the case at all? What if the poison had been added to the wine when it was corked below stairs, and sent up to *le vicomte*? This possibility spurred her across the lawn toward the rear door where all Anne's hats hung. She would ask Monsieur Chouinard if he—

Then her steps slowed. But after opening the bottle for the master of the house, he couldn't very well offer any of the wine to the other guests. Wouldn't it be remarked upon if the butler hurried away with a nearly full bottle? He would have to drop it, and nothing so spectacular had happened. He had simply poured a glass for her.

Bother. She was just going to have to work her way through her list, and resign herself to the fact that it was not going to be easy. If only she had one of those machines she'd heard whispers of in parlour gossip about the Walsingham Office. The Veritas Device. One's hand was strapped inside it, and questions were asked. Out the other end came a tape bearing something like Morse code, not recording the answers, but instead one's reaction to the questions.

A liar always had a tell. Her late husband's had been to finger his watch chain. Georgia had already known that at least one of the charms on that chain had been another woman's gift. Perhaps he had been invoking her in some way as he had lied through his teeth about where he had been, or what he had been doing. Eventually it had become pointless to ask, for Georgia would never get the truth.

Perhaps that was one of the reasons Dustin Seacombe's company was so calming. Well, when he wasn't driving her distracted with that gravelly voice and those dark eyes. He always spoke the unvarnished truth, no matter how irritating. It was a policy she had always employed with Teddy, too. She would not speak ill of his father, but Teddy had been quick enough to understand how much one could say with silence.

She came to herself at the side of a canal, gazing into its clear depths with a sense of surprise. She had been so deep in thought she had almost walked straight off the bank.

"May I help you, madame?" The male voice came from right behind her and she gasped. The toes of her shoes met thin air and she teetered on the bank, her arms cartwheeling for balance. He seized her around the waist and she shrieked as he dragged her back.

"Madame! A thousand pardons, I did not mean to startle you. Are you all right?" He let her go, a safe six feet away from the steep drop into the canal.

She wheezed—turned—and recognized him. "Monsieur Martin!"

"Please forgive me." He pulled his battered felt hat from his head and crushed it in his distress. "The fault is all mine. I should have hailed you from a greater distance."

The years of his education in Scotland with Gregory had given his accented English an appealing burr. Georgia's breath evened out and she hastened to assure him she was all right. "I did not realize I was so close to the edge. I have been out walking and thinking … and not looking where I was going."

"Come. There is a bench just here. Please rest for a moment."

After shrieking at him as though he were a murderer, poor man, the least she could do was accept his invitation. The bench sat in the welcome shade of an ancient elm, and she sank onto one end while he took the other. He sat as though glad to take some weight off his bad leg.

"I was looking for Monsieur Laurent, but then I fell into a reverie," she explained, feeling as silly as she sounded.

"In his absence, may I be of assistance?"

Unless you can divine who poisoned your friend, unfortunately not. But she could not say such things aloud. "I think you said the last time we spoke that you had known Gregory Campbell for some years?"

If he thought this an odd answer to his polite question, he did not show it. "Since our first year at Cambridge. We were both in the School of Engineering, both transferred to the applied mechanics side of it in Edinburgh for our graduate work." He smiled at something in the distance of memory. "He was much more clever than I, so when he offered me this position with the proviso that the operation of his massive irrigation project was part of it, I jumped at the chance."

"And what did your family think of a move to France?"

"My mother encouraged it. My father passed some years

ago." He glanced at her. "As for a wife or children, I have neither. Until I took my position here, I had not been the best marriage prospect."

"Then the women of your acquaintance are fools," Georgia blurted, then blushed. "I beg your pardon. That was presumptuous of me."

"It is quite all right. Compliments do not come my way so often than I can consider them anything but welcome."

"Do you know Gregory's cousins well?"

He shook his head. "I met Roger once when I spent a school holiday with Gregory. I confess it was all too easy to leave him behind during our adventures in the woods. He would trip over a rock, and spend the next hour digging it up, not to clear the path but to see what it was made of."

"So his love of geology began early."

"That it did. As did ours, first with clocks and mechanical devices, then the construction of machines."

"Did he ever quarrel with his cousin? Was there any animosity between them?"

"I only saw Roger the once. He was younger than we were. You know boys of that age. We were always trying to lose him so that we could go into the town, or go fishing, and not have to look after him. I see now how it might have become a chip on his shoulder—being left out. We might have been kinder."

"Did it spoil their relationship in the present? My aunt and I did not arrive soon enough to observe them together. And then …" Her voice trailed away.

Monsieur Martin gave this some thought. She wondered if he thought her rude for prying into his friend's personal affairs. If he did, he politely kept it to himself.

"I wouldn't say their relationship was spoiled, exactly," he said at last. "I am not the most observant of men, but I did sense a little of that childhood resentment now and again. He would insist on accompanying Gregory and me out to the pumps, even though he is clearly not the mechanical sort. It was more like he had determined not to be left behind on an errand that was important to us." He glanced at her. "Two of the pumps had been disabled. Once he had made his point, though, he felt free to spend his time on what he preferred. He and Sibyl have made quite a study of the geology of these cliffs."

Georgia had no time for geology. "The pumps had been disabled? Were they under repair?"

A smile flashed and was gone. "They were once we found out why the water levels in the third ring had dropped so precipitately. They had been damaged on purpose. By someone who did not know what they were doing, and considered brute force the means to achieve their aims."

"What was their aim? Did you find out who it was?"

"Their aim was to divert the water to the Villiers acres instead of through the town. What they did not understand is that the irrigation system on that ring was designed by Gregory and Stefan do both. Luckily we were able to make the repairs before the townsfolk found their steam boilers had no pressure, and their plumbing no water."

"How dreadful." Villiers again. "Did *le vicomte* bring this lapse in judgement to Monsieur Villiers' attention?"

"Oh, yes. Repeatedly. And each time he was assured that the matter had been taken care of. Both of us knew that his hydraulics man is a buffoon. But he is Villiers' brother-in-law and he will not sack him."

Another motive for getting Gregory out of the way and a

more tractable, less intelligent heir installed in his place. Was Stefan Villiers capable of such a thing?

"I will say that Roger's help was welcome on that occasion," Monsieur Martin went on. "With the three of us and two men from my staff, we had both pumps repaired that same morning. One of my young men grew up on the canals before they were improved. Gregory observed that he had talent, and felt he should be encouraged in his education. I had the feeling that he was willing to contribute to that end." He sighed. "Now I suppose the poor boy will have to fend for himself."

"You will encourage him," Georgia said. "And if that is what he really wants, he will find a way."

"You are an optimist, I see."

"As are you, or you would not be here." A little silence fell. At length Georgia asked, "With your friend's passing, what will you do?"

He lifted one shoulder in a way that was so French, Georgia was reminded that indeed, he was. "The estate must be carefully managed now more than ever. Vigilance is always needed for the irrigation system. When *la vicomtesse* is once again able to take the reins of the estate, I will be here to support her." He leaned back, his damaged hand clasped in the other. "I have observed that the twins Elodie and Eloise have a natural affinity for clocks and mechanical devices, to say nothing of water. Their governess has told me that in learning to work the compasses for their lessons, they began by drawing the concentric rings of the irrigation system. They must have seen their father's drawings. I cannot imagine where else they would have apprehended such a thing."

"Perhaps they have been up on the roof of the chateau,"

Georgia suggested. "The system can be seen clearly from up there. And from the air on approach, of course, it is very much apparent—the first thing one notices after the turrets of the chateau become visible."

He nodded, his mouth giving the downturn of a man impressed. "Perhaps they will be the next Campbells to plague the Dean of Engineering at the University of Edinburgh."

"I do hope so. It would be wonderful to think of them carrying on their father's legacy." But she must return to the more immediate demands of their father's death. "Monsieur Martin, may I confide in you?"

"Of course, madame." His gaze settled on her with all the gravity of a man taking an oath. "Whatever you tell me will go no farther."

"You were Gregory's closest friend," she began slowly, feeling her way toward the words that must shock, but at the same time might give clarity to this awful situation. "And I am Anne's oldest friend. I feel obligated to share with you what Millie and I have recently learned about his death."

"Recently?" Perhaps he was wondering if two ladies of a certain age had been poking about where they shouldn't in the catacombs. "How is that possible?"

"After some investigation conducted by the two of us, Millie consulted with Doctor Besson, and together they confirmed our suspicion that Gregory did not die of a heart attack. Or rather, he did, but it had been induced. By means of poison."

He went so still that she wondered if he was even breathing. The only thing that moved was the color draining from his face.

"Monsieur, shall I fetch you some water?"

With a gasp, he came to himself. "No, indeed. I am well. That explains it." She waited for him to recover, and go on. "I *knew* he had no heart condition. I could not understand it, a man as healthy and young as he. What poison?"

"Root of monkshood. Taken, we believe, from the kitchen garden."

"There is a plant containing such virulent poison in the kitchen garden?" At this fresh shock, he flushed with anger. "What if the children were to run in there and pick it?"

"Madame Laurent is very vigilant."

"Ah yes. The cleaver incident. That would also explain her disrespectful behavior to *la vicomtesse*."

"I believe now that she was trying to prevent Anne from touching any of those plants. Millie says the entire back corner is a poison garden. Some have medicinal uses, but I cannot see any use for monkshood but ... the one it was put to."

"And you have proof?"

"If botany texts, Anne's own testimony of what happened in the small hours of the night, and the doctor's concurrence are proof, then yes, we do."

He sat back with a sigh, clearly still coming to grips with this appalling news.

"I have urged Anne to summon the *gendarmes* to find the person responsible, but she has forbidden it," Georgia said into a silence broken only by birdsong and the ever-present whisper of water in the canal. "So Millie and I are making the attempt."

Any other man, with the possible exceptions of Mr Seacombe and Mr van Meere, would have guffawed at worst, and tried to dissuade her at best. But Benezet Martin did neither. She could practically see the cogs turning in the powerful engine of his mind.

"Now I see the direction of all your previous questions," he said at last. "I will not insult your intelligence by urging you to be careful in your inquiries."

"Thank you." A smile of appreciation flickered at the corners of her mouth. "You will be happy to know that you are not on our list. If you had wanted to do away with your friend, you would have found ample opportunity over the years. But more important, his trust in you may be trusted by us all, I think."

Color flooded his face more deeply. "I am honored."

"The question that has been nagging at me this afternoon is not so much *who* as *how*. I think that once we can determine *how* the poison was administered, it will narrow down the list of who might have done the administering."

"The night of his birthday party." The mental gears engaged, and Georgia couldn't help but hope that, like the tape coming out of a Veritas Device, ideas might come out of Monsieur Martin's mouth that would give her a direction to pursue that as yet she and Millie had not thought of.

"The poison can take anywhere from two to six hours to do its work, Millie says," she offered. "When we were on the terrace before dinner, he was already trembling. Unsteady. And by the time we were seated in the dining room, he said he could not feel his mouth."

"Which suggests the poison was administered before the guests arrived, in food or drink. For he died little more than six hours later."

"The question Millie and I have been turning over is … what food or drink? And when?"

"It has been some days since that evening, Lady Langford. Any clues that might have been touched or left behind are gone. The staff pride themselves on habits of cleanliness and elegance."

"I have never seen that as a drawback until now," Georgia admitted. "People permitted entrance to the poison garden number only two—Monsieur and Madame Laurent."

"It can be accessed without permission, of course. Gates are left unlocked, walls can be scaled, kitchens can be entered."

What a depressing thought. "The only members of the staff to whom I have spoken are Mademoiselle Boyle and yourself. Madame Fleury says she has not been in the kitchen garden since she was a child. And Roger Campbell could not identify monkshood. In fact, he cannot tell a delphinium from a hollyhock."

"They say poison is a woman's weapon," he said carefully.

She stepped on to this well-worn track without effort. "I have heard the same. What do you know of Sibyl Campbell?"

"She tended to be away at school when I visited, but on the one occasion she happened to be home, she was much occupied with her circle of acquaintance, making calls with her mother, that sort of thing."

"No tagging after you and Gregory?"

"Not unless it involved rocks."

"So early? Was she as mad for them as her brother?"

"She is mad for order. She was the official recorder of information about his collection. Who carefully made specimen boxes and labels. To this day she writes the articles to which he puts his name, though when they present their discoveries at conferences, they do it together."

"And what sort of relationship did she have with their cousin?"

"Cordial, as far as I know. Though it was rather taken for granted that Roger would be his heir after the girls' birth. Gregory, as the elder of the two male great-grandchildren, inherited a small estate from his Scottish grandparents, and heir or no heir, it belongs now to Roger. It was not until after Gregory acceded to the French title that they learned about the role of the Court of Inheritance and the dusty corridors of French law."

"So Sibyl did not aspire to being the châtelaine here at Roger's side?"

"The only aspirations she has, to my knowledge, are to see her own name on a monograph. Goodness knows she can do it. He may have a nose for fossils, but her knowledge of them is greater."

Georgia turned over this information in silence. "It does not seem likely that either of them would jeopardize their careers over a chateau, especially in a country not their own whose language they refuse to speak."

"I tend to agree. Though if Anne does not bear a son in the autumn, everything will depend on the ruling of the Court. Roger may yet emerge with both career *and* chateau, and be forced to expand his horizons."

CHAPTER TWELVE

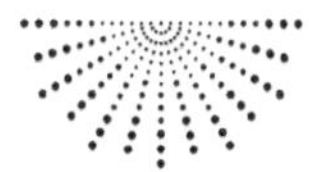

But Roger's expectations were not Georgia's concern. "Another name is floating to the top of our list. What do you know of the priest?"

Monsieur Martin's eyebrows rose. "Père François? You suspect him?"

"At this point, I suspect nearly everyone in the parish," she said. "We have heard that François was quite the vengeful bully before he entered the church. The lads in Valmy were apparently afraid of him."

"Vengeance is mine; I will repay, saith the Lord," Monsieur Martin said in a low, thoughtful tone, almost like a warning.

Georgia felt a tingle of surprise at his quick connection. "Exactly. But what I have not yet discovered is whether this trait has been suppressed by the love of God, or whether Gregory committed some offense that brought it rushing to the surface in this act of violence."

Monsieur Martin frowned at the daisies in the grass at their feet. "But poisoning, strictly speaking, is not violent. It takes place at a remove, once the substance has been administered."

"We agree on the narrow window of time in which it could have been done."

"But in that window, was not Père François in the drawing room with the other guests?"

And here she was again, trying to remember who had been there. The priest's cassock had made him stand out, though. She had noticed him as she had entered the room. "Yes, he was. But I do not know how long he had been there, since we arrived later."

"There I can help. I met him in the path to the senior staff cottages."

"Cottages?" Georgia had seen no other outbuildings from the roof. She would have remembered cottages, surely.

"Yes, the Laurents live in one, and I in the other. The chapel lies on one side, and there is a belt of woods running behind. I met François in the path, presumably coming from the chapel, and we walked up to the chateau together. We were some of the first to arrive."

She let out a long breath. "So unless he slipped Gregory the poison in the communion cup at chapel before his party, he cannot have done it."

"I would say not, since to my knowledge Gregory and Anne were in the house, preparing for their guests."

Georgia conjured up her list in her mind and drew a line through the name *Père François*. "How unfortunate. I was beginning to like vengeance as a motive. Though for what, I do not know."

He chuckled. "Don't sound so disappointed. There is still money, power, and love."

"And the greatest of these is love," she murmured.

"Is it?" He looked a little startled.

She shook her head, embarrassed at having spoken aloud. "Now that you have me suspecting the neighbors, do you think the motive of money applies to Stefan Villiers?"

He almost shook his head, then stopped himself. "A month ago, I would have said no and believed it completely. But after the debacle with the pumps, I can no longer be sure. I went with Gregory to speak to him, as I said, and while Gregory accepted his word as that of a gentleman, I could not entirely do so."

"Why not?"

He frowned again at the daisies. "He did not seem entirely sincere in his assurances. Especially since all three of us knew that his brother-in-law was entirely capable of damaging the pumps."

"Then I shall speak to him, and see if he is hiding something. I am going to invite him and his wife to dinner Wednesday. Perhaps you would like to join us?"

Monsieur Martin chuckled. "You will not get a word out of him if I am there. He will be in … how do you say it? A high dudgeon. I am, you see, merely a lowly estate agent."

Georgia leaned away to inspect his face for evidence he was joking. Finding none, she shook her head. "You are a gentleman, sir, by both education and breeding. If he treats you as anything less, then I have lost all regard for him."

"That is kind of you, Lady Langford. But these men come from old families, and old habits die hard. Dining with one's peers is one of them. I might join their hunt and shoot the pheasant or the deer meant for dinner, but I may not join them to eat it."

That was a Blood sentiment if ever she had heard one. Goodness. France was so modern and civilized in some ways, and so dreadfully behind the times in others. Did they have conflicts between Blood and Wit ideas here, too?

But she had already taken up too much of his day, so she would not open that discussion. Instead, she rose, and he rose with her. "Thank you for your help, monsieur. You have given me food for thought."

"I am glad. I wish you *bonne chance* with your inquiries. If I can be of assistance in even the smallest way, please let me know. *La vicomtesse* would wish it, and I stand ready to do anything that will ease the pain of her loss and bring her and the children peace."

"I will." She held out her hand, and he clasped it in strong fingers.

They parted ways, she to make her way to *Helena* to write down what she had learned while it was still fresh in her mind, and he to the duties from which she had kept him. The sun lay like the hand of a friend upon her shoulders.

A friend. She sighed as she walked up the gravel avenue to the airfield. If Dustin Seacombe were here right now, what would he make of all this? Well, she knew what *she* made of the estate agent's parting words. If Benezet Martin was not pining with unrequited love for Anne Campbell, she would eat one of Anne's straw hats.

The problem was, despite her show of confidence in him a few minutes ago, did that make him *more* likely to do away with his best friend for Anne's sake? Or less?

～

MILLIE HAD NEVER BEEN SO thankful for a sun hat and reliable walking boots in all her life. The climb down the cliffs had not been so bad, thanks to a clear path, but the walk along the shingle to the cliffs that bore the specimens had been taxing. And very warm.

Her hosts had even left her behind in their eagerness to find a good specimen for her. She came up behind them in time to hear Roger say, "This layer isn't the *Dalle aux Ammonites*, old girl, but we may find one or two. Enough for the old lady and for a paper, wouldn't you say?"

"I'm so sorry, Miss Brunel," Sibyl said brightly, turning as Millie came up. "We didn't mean to come ahead so fast. I am afraid the ammonites exert a call as strong as that of any siren."

Millie had been called worse than *old lady*. And her purpose would not be served by their knowing she had heard them. "How did you find these in the first place?"

"The girls showed us when we first arrived," Sibyl said. "I must say, I was worried their carelessness would damage the specimens before we could unearth them."

"Chased them off, in no uncertain terms," Roger said, extracting a small pickaxe from his rucksack.

"This is their property," Millie pointed out. "They are free to go where they like, I should think."

"Scientific inquiry takes precedence," Roger said. "Believe me, if this estate winds up in my hands, I shall take great care that no one trespasses here. No more sailboat races. Imagine crowds milling about on this beach, destroying specimens millions of years old." With the pickaxe, he attacked what looked like a round, flattened lump.

"Speaking of trespassing," Millie said, "I was saddened to

learn that the kitchen garden at the house is out of bounds. I had a great desire to try my hand at making lavender lemonade. Lavender we have a-plenty, but lemons are only to be found where I am told angels fear to tread."

"Just ask the cook for one," Sibyl suggested. "You don't have to go out there and pick it yourself. Better yet, ask her to make a jug of lemonade and bring it to you."

"Ah, but then I should never learn to make it. And if we fly to Gibraltar or Italy or some other hot place, I should have to do without."

"Sibyl, are you going to stand there nattering, or have a go at this fellow?"

At once his sister extracted what looked like an ice pick and a small brush, and commenced to scrape away the rubble her brother had created. The specimen now lay partly exposed.

"Anyway, it's not true that the garden is forbidden," Roger said, the *tink!* of his tool on the rock competing with the rolling movement of the stones down at the tide line and the mewing of gulls. "I've seen people in there. My room, y'know. Looks right down into it."

Possibility tingled along Millie's veins. She peered at the specimen with her best impression of keen interest. "Do you remember who? I might need a co-conspirator in my quest for lemons."

"Don't know exactly. Herself, of course. Her husband, quite often. Some young woman a week or two ago. That tall, lanky footman who doesn't know his place. Going to sack that one if I inherit."

He had to mean Jean-Pierre, who did not suffer fools

gladly. "What young woman, Mr Campbell? Not Valerie, Anne's lady's maid, surely?"

"Why would she be in the garden?" *You silly old biddy*, she heard as clearly as if he'd said it. "Some other chit. In a delicate condition—about ready to drop her foal."

He struck the extracted lump smartly on its edge and it cracked in half, exposing a glossy ammonite the size of her palm.

"It's just a baby." She was hardly aware of what she said, so startled was she at the news of another person with access to the poison garden. She must find out who she was at once. A woman expecting a child so imminently should not be difficult to identify.

"*Coroniceras multicostatum* could grow up to twenty-eight inches across," Sibyl told her. "You may be right that it died quite young, and fell to the seabed. Would you like to know how it got from the bottom of the sea to this cliff?"

Heaven forbid. "I—I'm sorry." She put a hand to her forehead. "I think I have had too much sun. I would like to return to the house, if I may."

"Certainly." Sibyl turned back to the excavation. Roger did not appear to have heard. So much for an escort, not that Millie would have appreciated it. "Careful on the path."

"Thank you for finding the fossil for me."

But neither were listening. They were already discussing how best to get a larger one out of its resting place and into their collection.

Having no pockets in her skirt, Millie cradled the fossil in her palm and used the other hand to help herself up the cliff path, resolutely keeping her eyes on the way before her and not the distance straight down to the waves purling in on the beach.

"I hope you get caught by the tide and have to swim," she told the Campbell siblings politely over her shoulder.

She emerged at the top of the cliff not far from the stone edifice that marked the entrance to the catacombs, and set off through the wildflowers to the house. Who might know who the mysterious girl was? She dared not interrupt anyone in the kitchen—it was nearly time for lunch, and Madame Laurent's troops would be moving like a finely tuned machine.

Then she caught sight of a battered straw hat moving above the privet hedges that formed the patterns in the rose garden. She slipped in through the gate, lost herself for ten minutes in the mazes formed by the hedges' patterns, and followed the sound of clippers back the way she had come.

Monsieur Laurent looked up at the sound of her footsteps crunching in the white gravel, and set aside his clippers. Carefully, he gathered up a double handful of hedge trimmings and placed them on a square of burlap sacking. "Are you enjoying the garden, madame?"

"I am, very much." She breathed in the scent of the roses and the cut privet as she tried to slow her breathing after her gallop up to the house. "Have you no assistant to help you keep the gardens so beautifully? I thought I saw you just minutes ago, trimming the ivy on a wall."

He smiled, his deeply tanned face nearly the color of the soil itself. An indigo scarf was knotted about his neck, and over his shirt he wore a waistcoat of heavy linen, stained with soil, in whose pockets were smaller tools and—she peered at it —a tiny seedling. Some kind of tree.

He followed her gaze. "I must transplant this little one soon. I am trying to decide on the best place for it, since it is an elm and will grow nearly as tall as one of our towers."

"Perhaps near the gates on the road? I saw a fallen tree there. You must have had a dreadful storm this past winter."

"A good suggestion, madame." He patted his pocket. "I bid you a good day."

"One moment, monsieur," she said hastily. "I heard there was a young woman in the kitchen garden not long ago. I had been hoping to pick a lemon or two. Do you know her? Does she sell them in the market?"

Whether or not he thought this question exceedingly odd, he merely shook his head. "That would have been our granddaughter, Hortense. She came now and again for certain herbs and flowers, which she compounded for the apothecary in Valmy."

"Your granddaughter," Millie said a little flatly. That did not sound like an ideal suspect, though the apothecary part held promise.

"That must have been some time ago, though, madame. Hortense has not been here in more than two weeks—she was recently brought to bed of a child, who did not survive." His face seemed to crumple. "And she is not recovering from the birth. I am worried." He checked himself. "But of course you will not wish to be burdened with our troubles."

Compassion rose like a wave in Millie's heart. "It is no burden, monsieur. The burden is in bearing our troubles in silence, when there are friends to help. How old is your granddaughter?"

"She is nearly seventeen." He lifted his head proudly. "She was married young, I know, but her husband is a stonemason, and is good to her. He repaired many of the walls after the late vicomte came."

A funeral mass. A baby boy. "It is for him the masses are being celebrated?"

He nodded, and dashed the dampness from his eyes.

"I am so very sorry. Is there anything I can do for you or madame?"

His gaze held all the sorrow of the ages, and the country-man's knowledge that while this, too, might pass, it would not be forgotten. "If you would pray for Hortense, madame, it would be a kindness. Doctor Besson has done all he can and more. It is up to God now."

She gripped the ammonite and made up her mind. "I shall go at once to the chapel and light a candle for her. Please let Madame Laurent know that if Hortense needs anything at all, she is to call upon me and Lady Langford. If it is in our power, we will help."

His mouth trembled, and he nodded, the brim of his hat dipping low over his face.

She did not think he even noticed her hurry away. Only the slow sound of the clippers followed her out of the garden. Or it might have been the muffled gasps of a brokenhearted man.

The chapel dated from an age when private services were conducted for noble families, and formed part of the house. To Millie's mind, it was larger than the stone church at Langford, and much higher, with many more of the awe-inspiring narrow stained-glass windows for which France was known. She had been in here for Gregory's funeral, of course, but she had not been in a frame of mind that allowed for observation.

Not that there was much to observe here, except for the necessary actions she had promised Monsieur Laurent.

She lit a taper and placed it among the two dozen or so that burned in iron holders before the altar. Then, since there were no pews or kneeling cushions, she folded her hands around the ammonite and simply bowed her head to pray for the wellbeing of Hortense.

Several minutes later, she opened her eyes, breathed deeply of the sweet scent of beeswax, and strolled around the edges of the chapel. Churches were full of people and families and history, all of which she found interesting. Here were painted stone shields that echoed the one on Anne's stationery, with the deer and the hawk and the banner proclaiming DUCAT QUI PACEM CUPIT. Other shields, presumably of people who had married into the de Valmy family, had been mounted at intervals. Set lower down were plaques, some in bronze, some marble, and some in local stone, bearing the dates of birth and death of people Millie assumed had been employed on the estate. The plaques went up the wall as far as the eye could see—past the Napoleonic Wars into the medieval period.

A familiar name caught her eye much lower down. The Laurent dearly departed might be in the catacombs with their neighbors, but their plaques were grouped together between two stone pillars holding up the exterior wall near the double doors. Something unusual caught her eye, so she bent closer. Here were Monsieur and Madame Laurent with a plaque for themselves, bearing their names, dates of birth, and a blank space where each of their dates of death would go.

"Now, that is taking economy to the extreme," she

murmured. But theirs was far from the only stone carved in this manner.

Under their names were those of two sons who seemed to have died on the same day several years ago. Her pity for the grieving father over in the rose garden kindled again. And here was a girl's name with a date of death nearly seventeen years before.

Genevieve Laurent. There was no husband's name carved beside it.

Below that were Hortense's name, and that of her husband Joseph, with a space under them that had been inked where the carving had not yet been done.

Jean-Joseph Rivard, born and died
May 25, 1895

"Oh," Millie whispered. "Poor monsieur and madame. Three children gone, and a great-grandson, and now their granddaughter's recovery is uncertain. No wonder the poor man cannot hide his grief."

Her gaze returned to the names of Genevieve and Hortense. Genevieve's date of death matched Hortense's date of birth.

Genevieve had not been married. And had evidently died giving birth to the young woman who was even now in danger of the same fate. Had Genevieve had a lover who had deserted her on the news she was pregnant? Or had Hortense been the result of some dreadful act by a man whose name she would never know?

It was unlikely Millie would discover the answers. To ask Madame Laurent was unthinkable, and to ask her husband would be cruel. But what she could do was employ her limited knowledge of the uses of herbs to offer some help. It might be useless. The situation might have progressed too far, if even Doctor Besson had given up the case.

But she had to try.

3:25 p.m.

Millie had, of course, consulted with Madame Laurent before doing anything so rash as exercising her poor skills upon the woman's granddaughter. Madame had gazed at her with resignation. "Doctor Besson has tried everything, madame. I do not see how you can help."

"But I have one of the doctor's books, and an excellent library. I am not convinced I can help, either, dear madame, but something within me compels me to try."

Perhaps Millie's sincerity turned the tide. Madame had taken her list of ingredients into the kitchen garden, filled a basket, and then added a vial of brandy for the tincture. Millie had compounded the mixture, with the help of the two books, right there in the kitchen under her watchful eye. After which the woman had gone so far as to order the landau to convey Millie into Valmy with all possible speed.

Jean-Pierre was delighted to exercise his skills, and assured her he would deliver the message of her intentions to the doctor. When he returned, he would not stir from the door of Monsieur Rivard's home until she was ready to leave. Since Monsieur Rivard lived on the canal at the edge of town, the footman would likely take his time on the return, but Millie had bigger fish to fry than his social and flirtatious tendencies.

Monsieur Rivard was away at work, but a maid in a cotton apron admitted her, introduced herself as Lali, and escorted her back to a bright bedroom with whitewashed walls and curtains of the indigo blue so prevalent in the region. Her patient lay in a bed whose sheets were as white as the walls, her face as pale as milk.

"Madame," the maid said hesitantly. "Here is Madame Brunel to see you, from the chateau." When there was no response, the maid whispered, "Doctor Besson was here this morning, and changed the dressings. She is still bleeding."

Millie's heart went out to the young woman in the bed. Hardly more than a child, she looked as though she had given up on the prospect of life, and was simply … waiting.

"Would you take some water from the steam boiler," she whispered to the maid, handing her a stoppered bottle. "One part of this mixture to three parts hot water now, and another before bed. Three more tomorrow—morning, noon, and night."

"What is it, madame? Does the doctor know?"

"He does. It is a compound of several plants, but mostly Lady's Mantle."

Lali's eyes widened. "You are an herbwoman? A white witch?"

Millie needed a moment to gather her startled wits. "No indeed. But I have been reliably informed that it may help."

Lali hustled away to do her bidding, and Millie sat on the edge of a wicker chair that had been drawn up to the side of the bed. Though the wicker creaked loudly, the still form under the sheets did not move. "Hortense, my name is Millie. I do not know if anything I can do will help, but your grandmother has sent me with her blessing. When the tea comes, will you oblige me by drinking it?"

Hortense's lashes fluttered, and at last her eyes opened, her gaze fastened on the door as though she were expecting someone else. Then she rolled her head on the pillow to look at Millie.

If a live wire had been strung through Millie's body and a galvanic charge applied to it, the shock would have been no different than when her eyes met those of her patient.

Azure eyes. As clear and brilliant as the Mediterranean. As memorable as those of Gregory Campbell. But while his twin daughters possessed dark curls, skin like milk, and a widow's peak, this girl's hair was nut brown without a sign of a widow's peak, her nose freckled. But the eyes were the same.

"Madame?" The maid came in with the hot tea mixture, and Millie blinked and realized she had been staring in a silence as complete as Hortense's own. "It is hot, as you instructed."

With the maid's help, Millie lifted Hortense enough on her pillows so that she could drink the tea. All of it, despite the fact that she tried to turn her head away.

"My dear, you will have another of these before bed, and three more tomorrow. You must do your best to drink each cup. I shall come again the following day with more. It may be a fool's errand, but I have been called worse."

"Why should … you care?" Hortense whispered fretfully.

Why did she? There had not been time to ask herself that. "I have experienced so much death lately that I cannot bear any more. I am sorry to the core of my heart that you have lost your little boy. The doctor assures me that he has done everything he can for you, and I believe him. I am probably a fool, and a delusional one at that, but I cannot ignore what I feel. And your grandmother does not wish me to. She, you see, still finds it possible to hope."

The pale lips flickered with what could have been a smile … or a spasm of pain.

Millie leaned forward and kissed the cheek that should be glowing with new motherhood. "I will leave you to rest, and will return the day after tomorrow."

Hortense did not respond, but the maid looked up at her with wide-eyed respect. Millie knew, as this girl in the apron did not, that extracting the blessing of both Madame Laurent and the doctor did not mean she was worthy of anyone's respect.

Only that there was nothing left to try.

CHAPTER THIRTEEN

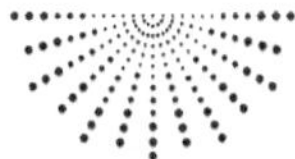

MONDAY, JUNE 3, AT 8:45 P.M.

Georgia had done her best to admire Millie's little ammonite, and Millie had listened to her theories about Stefan Villiers and the sabotage of the water system as they had dressed for dinner. But it was her news of Hortense that interested Georgia most.

Eyes the same color as those of Gregory? What could it mean? Something … or nothing?

"But in all other ways she bears no resemblance to him or his children," she pointed out, fastening her second earring. "Surely many people have eyes that color. Anne herself has grey eyes—until she puts on a green dress. Or a blue one. They are very changeable."

"Perhaps you are right." Millie did not wear earrings as a rule, except for the pearl clips she kept for special occasions, so she was waiting for Georgia at the door of her cabin. "But it did startle me. I wish I knew more about genetics. Perhaps the roots of the family go back a long way in this parish, and the eye color is unique to the area, not merely to Gregory."

"I think you have enough on your plate with your study of

botany. I salute you, dearest, for your efforts to help. That said, I do hope Madame Laurent is strong enough to bear … whatever happens in the next day or two."

"I do, too." Millie chewed her bottom lip, then said, "I have never felt a compulsion like this. It is probably compassion mixed with despair at the amount of death we have seen lately. But I could not refuse it, or convince it to go away with logic and sense."

"We are not scientists," Georgia said firmly. "We are not obliged to consort with logic and sense unless we wish to, or we are at the helm of our airship. Speaking of, have you checked the communications cage? I did this morning. I cannot think why Anne has not answered my letter."

"I did just now, and I can," Millie said. "I hope you have not offended her to the point where her letter, when it comes, invites us to leave her house forthwith and never trouble her with our presence again."

"Yes," Georgia said weakly. "That thought has occurred to me, but I did not want to entertain it further."

Together, they walked down to the chateau, where Georgia had set convention on its ear and invited Benezet Martin to join them. And why should she not? He had been Gregory's closest friend, and was already acquainted with Roger and Sibyl Campbell. Since they were now practically *en famille*, it seemed a courteous and natural thing to do.

And if either of the Mesdames Chouinard or Laurent objected, she would … would … well, she would think of something. Anne would not be best pleased if both her house-keeper and her famous cook departed her employ within a week because Georgia had breached the bounds of rank.

Fortunately, it did not occur to either of the Campbells to

object to the company of someone they knew. While scientists may have their snobberies—she had heard Roger's disdainful tone in speaking of the science of atmospheric mechanics, though she couldn't think why he should feel that way when every airship carried equipment invented by those who studied it—at least he and his sister were not social snobs.

The dining room, in fact, was much more congenial this evening than all the previous evenings put together.

"I was telling Lady Langford this afternoon about how easily you were distracted by rocks as a boy," Monsieur Martin said, clearly enjoying both his company and his Coquilles St Jacques.

"I like to be consistent," Roger said modestly. "I think we only shared one tutor at Cambridge, when I arrived for my first year and the two of you began your last. But it was the beginning of my serious pursuit of geology." He glanced at his sister. "And Sibyl's."

"Our parents, rest their souls, believed in education when talent was evident," Sibyl said, not so modestly.

"But then you and Gregory scampered off to Edinburgh, leaving us both to our own devices."

"Which was perfectly natural and acceptable," Sibyl finished. "Do you remember when Gregory's father told him to cancel his expedition to— Where was it?" She appealed to her brother.

"Expedition!" He snorted. "More like a grand tour."

"If memory serves, he was to take up an internship in Venice," Monsieur Martin put in. "To study the feasibility of mechanical dams in the lagoon."

"To ease the effects of the *acqua alta*?" Millie asked.

"Yes, madame. How clever of you to apprehend the connection so quickly."

"A friend educated me on the subject recently." She glanced at Georgia, who couldn't resist a smile.

"In any case, Gregory was not to go. Instead, he came here, to the chateau, where his father introduced him to his relations."

"You too, if memory serves," Roger said.

"I accompanied him, since I could visit my family at the same time. It was then, as young men, that we first began to imagine the possibilities for the region if the water could be convinced to adapt to a system of discipline."

"And what of you, Sibyl?" Georgia asked. "Did you come here as a young woman as well?"

"Not I." There was so much finality in her tone it was almost horror.

Roger chuckled. "She was destined for the marriage mart. Such a fuss when she insisted on taking up a summer teaching position in Yorkshire."

"A county famous for its fossils," Millie said, nodding wisely.

Sibyl smiled at her, the first sincere smile Georgia had seen. "Exactly. Having no interest in marriage or in the exploits of young men set loose in France, I spent my time much more profitably."

"Set loose! That we were," Roger said, waving his fork. "Benezet missed the whole thing, for he was with his family for the most part. It was the first time Gregory had ever been let out of the laboratory … and consequently the first time he ever fell in love."

"In love?" Now things were getting interesting. "He fell in love here, before he met Anne?"

"Oh, yes. I never knew who she was, exactly. But I did know, from hints he let drop, that they would never be permitted to marry."

"Why not?" Georgia could imagine several reasons. And thank goodness for them, or he would never have met and married Anne.

Roger glanced at the butler, standing at attention in his niche near the wine decanters. He lowered his voice. "She was the sort of girl a man might while away a summer with, not marry. Not of our class, you know. His father had made it clear to him that he expected him to marry well, so it could never have been more than a fling."

And then he had met Anne, and all his father's instructions and orders had gone out the window anyway. While she was a gentleman's daughter, and had been educated as well as Georgia or any other young woman at St Cecelia's Academy for Young Ladies, she had certainly not come with an estate and a deferential welcome at the local bank.

"What year would this have been, Mr Campbell?" Millie sounded rather as though she were musing out loud. "I am trying to place it, having only met *le vicomte* so recently."

Roger waved at Monsieur Martin. "Can you remember? So much water under the bridge, you know. I do remember it was your first year at Edinburgh. So that would have been … seventy-eight?"

"Eighteen seventy-seven, I believe," Monsieur Martin corrected him. "He and his father had words, and I remember he came to Nice and stayed with us until it was time to return to Edinburgh. He was miserable."

"That girl. No better than she should be, from all accounts, though I never heard it that way from him." Roger shook his head. "I didn't stay much longer. Too many long faces and hard words for me. I joined Sibyl in Yorkshire and had a grand lark among the fossils until it was time to go up to Cambridge. Hey, old girl? Our first paper came out of our two weeks there."

"It did indeed."

Our first paper. But Georgia supposed that Sibyl was used to her brother using the plural and taking credit in the singular.

Monsieur Chouinard refilled their glasses and then vanished through the baize door, while the footmen removed their plates. What seemed like a very long time later, dessert was brought in by the footmen and Madame Laurent herself, the desserts already plated and arranged on each of three trays.

As his was put before him, Roger asked, "What's this now? It looks like a meringue."

"It is called a Baked Alaska, monsieur," she replied calmly. "I have had the recipe from a colleague in New York. Frozen cream is concealed in meringue and baked—and yet, the iced cream does not melt."

"Impossible. I don't believe it." He scooped a little meringue away with his spoon, and peered inside. A deep purple sauce trickled out. "By St George's dragon, you're right! How do you manage it?"

"I am sworn to secrecy, monsieur," she said with the complacency of the expert. "I hope you all enjoy it."

Georgia did, very much. Her sauce turned out to be plum, the meringue lightly flavored with lime, and the iced cream itself utterly divine. She was perfectly willing to leave the secrets of its construction to madame, and enjoy it for its own sake. Across the table, Benezet Martin closed his eyes in momentary bliss.

When he opened them, he said, "My cooking skills are so inadequate that something like this seems conjured by the gods."

"When madame can set even the laws of physics at naught," Georgia said, "we must wonder if she has powers we know not of."

Madame Laurent and the footmen departed, her lips forever closed upon the truth, but a smile of satisfaction glinting in her eyes.

Tuesday, June 4, at 12:10 a.m.

"Lady Langford. Madame, please wake up. You must come immediately."

Georgia dragged herself out of the deep sleep she had just achieved what seemed like minutes ago.

"Lady Langford!"

A desperate note in the voice below the viewing port brought her upright, then out of her comfortable sleeping cupboard to snatch the dressing gown from its hook. She had gone to bed with the viewing port open to the warm air, angled outward about four inches on neat brass hinges that resembled sextants. As she peered down, tying the dressing gown closed, she saw one of the housemaids dancing from foot to foot in anxiety, a moonglobe in one fist.

"Delphine, what is it? What has happened?"

"It is Monsieur Campbell, madame. He is dead!"

Her knees went weak with shock. It was all she could do to grip the sill and will her knees to lock upright. "I will be out in five minutes."

What a lucky thing she had packed a corset that laced in front. Georgia flung on a shirtwaist and a plain skirt, dragged on a pair of stockings, and laced up her comfortable half-boots in a frantic hurry. Her hair could fend for itself—she had braided it before bed.

She opened the door to find Millie in the corridor, likewise dressed, her hair carelessly wound on top of her head with a tortoiseshell pick stuck through it. "I heard," she said simply.

Together they hurried down the gravel avenue with Delphine, who was barely able to speak coherently. "Mademoiselle C-Campbell came to fetch me. She heard a sound from her b-brother's room, but when she went in, he was d-dead. She sent me to w-wake you."

"Thank you for coming so quickly, Delphine." Georgia hurried across the grand hall to the staircase. "You may return to your bed."

"Send someone for Doctor Besson," Millie told the girl. "Jean-Pierre will do—tell him to go in the landau. It is fastest."

"Oui, madame."

They found Sibyl fluttering from her own bedroom door to that of her brother, whimpering in a way that told Georgia a full-scale roar of distress was imminent. She had seen it often enough in Teddy, after any more than half an hour with his father.

"Sibyl, breathe," she ordered as kindly as she could. "Another breath. Good. Now, tell me the facts in order, please."

The woman seemed to calm a little at the prospect of a task she knew how to do. "After dinner, Roger had been feeling rather bilious, so after you and Mr Martin went to your beds, he did so as well. I stayed awake making some notes about the specimens we found today—yesterday. I got into bed and was just dropping off when—"

She gasped, as though the facts were too much for her.

Georgia grasped her upper arms, and Sibyl's tear-filled, rather prominent blue eyes searched her face. Looking for comfort. To be told it could not be true. "I know it's hard, dear. But your initial observations are important before I go in."

"Yes," she whispered, swallowing hard. "Yes, of course. Well. I was just dropping off when I heard a sound from Roger's room."

"A cry of fear?" Millie asked. "A groan of pain?"

"Closer to the latter. I put on my dressing gown and went into his room with a moonglobe. I knew he should never have eaten those scallops, never mind a second helping. I bent over him to ask if he wanted some of his seltzer water, and saw— and saw—"

"Breathe."

Sibyl gasped once, and then again. "And saw him staring in that awful way. His face was livid, and there was—oh dear—"

She bolted into her room, and in a moment came the sounds of retching.

"Come," Georgia said to Millie, and pushed open Roger's door.

"Oughtn't we to—"

"We will. After we see what she has seen." Georgia could only hope her stomach was stronger.

Nine women out of ten would have gone to tend Sibyl no matter what Georgia said, but the tenth one was Millie, who was more observant than most. She took a deep breath and followed Georgia into the bedroom. A moonglobe glowed faintly on the carpet, so Georgia picked it up and shook it into brighter life once more.

They stood side by side at the bed, gazing down on what Sibyl must have seen. Roger lay on his right side, facing them, his face gray in the light of the little globe, his lips purple, his eyes staring. A tide of liquid had soaked into the pillow and sheets.

"He vomited blood?" Millie whispered.

"No … look." They bent closer to the sheets, the moonglobe in Georgia's hand hovering an inch above. "It is not scarlet. It is purple."

Purple, with partially ingested food bits. Georgia turned away, her mind moving at lightning speed. Did red wine turn purple in the stomach? He had had a fair quantity of that. And the sauce inside the Baked Alaska had been purple, as had the roasted beets chopped into the salad. She was fairly certain she was never going to enjoy any of those again.

From the open window came the sound of wheels on gravel, which spat as the pilot urged the landau out of the carriage house and through the stable yard at speed.

"Jean-Pierre," Millie said unnecessarily.

"There is nothing we can do here," Georgia said. "Let us give Sibyl what help we can, and get her back into bed. If she can cry herself to sleep, it will be a blessing."

A little feminine care and cosseting reduced Sibyl to tears, and she was finally able to curl up under the blankets as Georgia and Millie quietly closed the window and the door.

The landau puttered up the sweep to the front steps, where Georgia met Dr Besson as he climbed down, heavy-limbed with weariness. "I am glad Jean-Pierre did not have to search half the parish for you," she said, waving the footman on. "But I am sorry to call you out on such an errand. Roger Campbell is dead in his bed."

"*Mon Dieu*, what tragedy must you all face next?" The doctor followed her upstairs. "Please tell me you have not gone in to see him."

"We did, for all the good it did us. He seems to have vomited in his final moments."

Dr Besson said something under his breath that Georgia chose not to hear.

When they were all three ranged along the side of the bed, the doctor put his bag on the floor and examined the body briefly, clearly searching for signs of injury. Georgia and Millie turned their backs until he pulled up the sheet over Roger's stark face.

"Did he show signs of distress this evening?" Dr Besson finally asked.

"Not that we noticed," Millie said. "He was in good humor at dinner, telling stories of his and *le vicomte*'s misspent youth. He enjoyed Madame Laurent's dessert—which may be partly responsible for the purple color you see. It was Baked Alaska with a raspberry sauce."

"No, Millie—it was blueberry."

Millie blinked at her. "I am certain mine was raspberry."

"No matter what it was, it sounds appalling," the doctor grumbled.

Roger's lips had been stained purple as well. And something tapped at Georgia's memory like an insistent bird at the window.

"Doctor, Miss Campbell told us before you arrived that Roger had complained of feeling bilious after dinner, and went straight up to bed. She woke when she heard a sound, and came in to offer seltzer water, only to find him dead."

"Bilious." He gazed at her. "He was not suffering from indigestion?"

So his mind was running on the same track as hers. Millie drew in a long breath that told Georgia hers had done the same. "Doctor," she said, "what if …" Her voice trailed away, as if to speak the words would make them true.

"There is only one way I can think of to test for juice of monkshood," he said in a voice only just audible.

He pulled down the sheet and dipped a finger in the purple liquid drying on Roger's lower lip. Georgia's stomach threatened to sacrifice her dinner as well when he dabbed a drop of the liquid on his own lip.

A moment later he whirled and strode for the water closet, where they heard the sounds of vigorous scrubbing. When he emerged, no telltale sign of purple was on his mouth.

"Blueberry sauce. My lip went numb," he said. "I hope the poison did not take hold. I scrubbed it off as soon as I felt it."

"Dear heaven." Millie sank onto the chest at the end of the bed.

In the absence of anywhere else to sit, Georgia gripped the bedpost to hold herself up and attempted to marshal her scrambled thoughts past the wall of fear. "How is this possible?" she whispered. "Why is this happening? And why cannot we stop it?"

"Mesdames, please. Let us discuss this elsewhere." The

doctor led them from the bedroom, and would have begun opening doors along the corridor to find a suitable room, but Georgia stopped him.

"There is only one place to discuss anything in safety. Please come aboard *Helena*."

"Your airship?" His voice rose a little in disbelief.

"Shhh. You will wake Miss Campbell, and we have only just got her to sleep," Millie whispered. "Come."

Five minutes later, the three of them were settled in the saloon, dimly lit by a single lamp in its sconce and the waxing moon traveling slowly into the west.

"Now," Dr Besson said, "tell me what time dinner was served, and what you saw anyone ingest beforehand."

"Dinner was *en famille*, at seven o'clock, with only ourselves, the Campbells, and Monsieur Martin at the table," Georgia began.

"Benezet Martin?" the doctor repeated in surprise. "To dinner at the chateau? With you?"

"Yes. He has known the Campbells since they were all young, at university. Since there was no need for formality, I invited him." She gazed at him. "I do not think the staff would be so offended as to resort to poison, however. Then Monsieur Martin or I would have been the victim, not Mr Campbell."

"Georgia, this is hardly the time for levity," Millie murmured.

"I am completely serious. There must be a motive for this. We just cannot see it."

"Dinner was at seven o'clock, and he was discovered by his sister ... when?"

"I do not know, but the maid Delphine came here to wake me at ten minutes past twelve."

He blinked at her owlishly. "You sleep here? When there are at least six guest bedrooms in the chateau?"

"With all the relations here for *le vicomte*'s funeral, we gave up our rooms and somehow never managed to return," Millie said. "We do not feel safe in the chateau."

"I should not, either. So before seven o'clock, where was everyone?"

"We gathered on the terrace for a glass of wine, then went in to dinner," Georgia said. "Millie and I had that lovely golden wine *le vicomte* was so proud of, and the Campbells and Monsieur Martin drank the red."

"With no ill effects, I assume."

"None. Following which, we ate from the same dishes, serving ourselves, and again drank the same wine. As you see, at least three of us survived the dinner itself. Though I would like to know if Monsieur Martin is feeling well."

"I will stop by his house to ask him when we are finished here," Dr Besson said.

"Wait," Millie said, holding up a hand. "We did not serve ourselves the dessert. It came in with some ceremony, with Madame Laurent herself and two footmen bearing the Baked Alaska on silver trays. They were baked in round shallow ramekins, and served to us individually. Apparently each with a different sauce."

Georgia drew a breath. "If the monkshood was in only one dessert, then it would have to be served with particular attention by the poisoner to their intended victim. There could be no room for error."

The doctor seemed to be struggling for words. Then he

blurted, "You are not suggesting that Madame Laurent, who is celebrated from here to the Loire for her culinary skills, poisoned *le vicomte* and then his cousin—the latter a man unknown to her prior to this visit?" Dr Besson appeared to have lost all respect for Georgia's intellect.

She must not grow defensive, or lose her patience. She must work through this in a calm, logical manner. "I suggest only that we keep an open mind. We have means and opportunity, but I confess that any possible motive eludes me."

"The only thing connecting the two men is that one inherited the chateau, and the other was one of the candidates to inherit it should *la vicomtesse* not produce a son in the autumn," Millie said. "But why that should incense the cook—celebrated or not—is a mystery. The first was a fair and kind employer. The second may have been unknown to her, but if she did not like the prospect of working for him, she could simply take up one of the many offers she could entertain, and leave."

The doctor remained silent.

Millie went on, "I do not believe Madame Laurent is the culprit. It would take a woman of exceptional *sangfroid* to present a poisoned dessert to her victim in front of so many witnesses."

"From what we have seen of her, it is rather clear her temper runs hot and hasty, not cold and calculated," Georgia agreed. "I think we must look elsewhere for our poisoner. We still have not eliminated Stefan Villiers. Perhaps we may do that Wednesday, when we expect them to dinner."

"Madame!" the doctor exclaimed. "Surely you are not serious. Monsieur Campbell is barely cold. The house will be plunged into double mourning, and no company admitted until after the funeral."

"But he will not be buried here." Georgia's cheeks felt hot at this reproof, though she had done nothing to be ashamed of except be unfamiliar with local custom.

"It does not matter. There can be no company, or there will be a storm of talk in the town."

Dr Besson had been their ally up until now, so Georgia bit back her remarks about the necessity of one's finding a murderer taking precedence over social expectation. This was not her home, but she was in charge of it until Anne's return. She must behave as Anne would, and show respect where it was due.

"Forgive me, Doctor. Of course you are right. I shall rescind my invitation. When they are aware of the reason, I am certain we will be forgiven."

"May we pay a call on the Villiers, then?" Millie asked.

"Usually one sends a tube to inform people of a death," he allowed. "But sending a representative to pay a call is seen as a mark of respect, especially between landowners."

"Then we will do so," Millie said.

In a softer tone, Georgia asked, "Will you again make the arrangements for burial, Doctor?"

Millie shifted on the sofa. "Doctor, have you by chance seen Hortense Rivard?"

"Yes. I looked in this evening. There is no change."

"But she is not worse?"

"She seems to be holding her own. You have dosed her with your concoction?"

"She will have had two doses yesterday, and three more today—morning, noon, and night. Then I shall take her more."

"As I said when you approached me, it cannot hurt the poor child now." The doctor sighed. "I had best be on my way. The mayor will have to be informed, and the priest. Along with Monsieur Martin, they will not thank me for waking them, but it must be done."

As Georgia pulled the lever to lower the gangway, he cleared his throat. "You will keep me apprised of your efforts to locate the person responsible for these deaths? And it goes without saying that you will be as discreet as possible?"

"Yes on both counts," Georgia assured him.

They watched him down the avenue, where the landau and Jean-Pierre were waiting in the sweep.

"Now that we are alone," Millie said as the gangway rose and locked into position, "what do you really think?"

Georgia walked slowly into the saloon, and she and Millie sat where they had been, on the sofa. "I think a busy cook does not make a complicated dessert with different sauces inside just to show off. Why not the same sauce in all?"

"Because then they could not be told apart," Millie said. "And she had to be able to tell which was the poisoned one."

"But we still do not know *why*." Georgia rubbed her temples, where a headache was forming. "Madame as our suspect does not make sense. Stefan Villiers does. He has motive in spades."

"But not means or opportunity … in the case of Roger Campbell, anyway."

So maddeningly true. "I do not want to think of *two* people at large in the chateau with intimate knowledge of the poison garden. But we cannot discount that possibility, either."

"Stefan killed Gregory, and then someone else with a

grudge against Roger killed him?" Millie's voice was laced with disbelief.

"Maybe his sister had had enough of being pushed aside and her efforts rewarded with nothing but stolen credit," Georgia said. "Maybe she decided to put an end to it."

"If this were the case, I would find it difficult not to sympathize," Millie admitted. "But again, Sibyl was not in the kitchen dribbling juice of monkshood root into the Baked Alaska. The entire staff would have seen it, and Madame would certainly have chased her out with the cleaver."

"Perhaps she paid Madame to do it."

Millie shook her head. "Both women have reputations and careers to lose. I do not see either of them taking such a risk. Georgia, you look positively pained. When was the last time you drank a glass of water?"

"This afternoon?"

Millie went to the galley and fetched her a large glass. "You know you need to drink more of this. Too little brings on your headaches."

She drank deeply, and in a few minutes was feeling more herself. "I am surprised Madame allowed you to mix up your Lady's Mantle mixture in her kitchen."

"It is her granddaughter I am trying to help," Millie pointed out. "The girl's situation may be grim, but as I told her yesterday, her grandmother clings to hope."

"Let us hope rather that Hortense recovers," Georgia said grimly. "Because until our poisoner is made to reveal him or herself, I do not want so much as a paring knife anywhere near you if madame's hopes should be dashed."

CHAPTER FOURTEEN

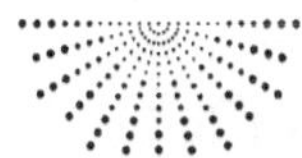

TUESDAY, JUNE 4, AT 7:45 A.M.

As temporary châtelaine, Georgia did not go down to the kitchen and embarrass Madame Laurent in front of all her staff. Instead, she seated herself in the morning room and sent for her.

The cook appeared in the doorway, her dignity drawn like a cloak about her.

"Do come in, madame." Georgia indicated the chair where Madame Chouinard normally sat to discuss the menus. "Thank you for being so prompt. I know you are busy preparing breakfast. But I must inform you that something dreadful has happened."

Madame nodded. "Monsieur Campbell. It is very sad."

Either Delphine or Jean-Pierre must have regaled the staff with the story already. Well, what was an hour here or there? They had to know.

"Miss Campbell, as you may imagine, is distraught. Could you prepare a tray for her? Something light but nutritious. She may not eat, but we can only try."

"Of course, madame." She rose as if to go.

Georgia lifted a hand. "A moment, if you please. My aunt and I consulted with the doctor about this new tragedy, and he has several questions. What can you share with me about last night's dessert?"

The woman seated herself slowly and gazed at Georgia, her brows crinkling in a puzzled frown. "I do not understand. I informed you and the guests that it was Baked Alaska. Iced cream with a meringue shell, baked quickly so that the iced cream does not melt."

"Yes, I remember. I must say that we enjoyed our dinner *en famille*, serving ourselves. None of us suffered any ill effects from the wonderfully prepared food."

Madame's head drew back in offense. "I should hope not."

Oh dear. Never mind. Press on. "However, the desserts were baked and served individually, each with a different sauce. Again, none of us became ill. Except Monsieur Campbell, who is dead. Madame, I must ask you—what was in the sauce inside his Baked Alaska?"

Now her mouth dropped open. A second later, she recovered herself and rose stiffly. "I will not subject myself to this."

"On the contrary, madame, you will. Please sit down."

If the air had been charged with lightning, it could not have felt more dangerous. Georgia knew from experience that if the cook did not obey, she would have to act. She was not looking forward to it. Instead, she concealed her emotion behind the aristocrat's expectant gaze. The one that always reduced the servants in her mother's house to sullen compliance.

It had the same effect now.

"I did not have enough varieties of compôte to fill five desserts, so yesterday I sent Jean-Pierre to the apothecary for a syrup of some other fruit or berry. He returned with blueberry, so I used it for the fifth dessert."

"Monsieur Campbell's dessert."

"It could have been anyone's. The desserts were not served according to preference. Are you telling me, madame, that the blueberry syrup was somehow tainted?"

"I am. Do you know what was in it?"

"*Non*, madame. The apothecary is not in the habit of affixing recipes to his concoctions. He prides himself on his exclusive cures and syrups and treats them all as a state secret."

"I see. Thank you, Madame Laurent. Please accept my apology for offending you. I did not mean my questions unkindly. We are all upset this morning."

A curt nod was all she received in return for this gracious effort, and madame rose and departed.

"If the quality of the food at Chateau de Valmy goes down, my girl, you have only yourself to blame," she muttered to the silent room. "But the questions had to be asked, as unsatisfactory as the answers were."

When Georgia recounted the conversation to Millie a few minutes later aboard *Helena*, she promptly agreed. "She was not about to tell you she had spiked the syrup with monkshood." Then, frowning, "Not that I think she did. You had a close call. She could have given her notice then and there."

"She may yet," Georgia said, burdened with the gloomy possibility of having to communicate such a disaster to Anne. "But I watched her closely. Her color did not change—she neither blushed nor paled, which one might think natural at practically being accused of murder. Her eyes did not lower, nor did she fidget. I think she was honestly so surprised at being asked about it that there was no room for guilt or outrage."

"I think we had better ask at the apothecary's shop, all the same," Millie said. "Leave no stone unturned and all that. I will go. I must take fresh tincture to Hortense."

They walked down to breakfast, only to find Sibyl at the table, dressed in a traveling suit of grey twill trimmed in black ribbon and addressing her plate in a businesslike fashion.

"My dear," Georgia said in surprise, "Madame Laurent was to have sent up a tray. Did it not arrive?"

"Oh, yes. But one little egg and some cut fruit will hardly sustain me the whole way."

"The whole … way?" Millie sounded mystified.

"To Paris."

Either she was going deaf, or poor Sibyl's mind had collapsed under this fresh family catastrophe. "I am sorry," Georgia said at last. "I do not understand."

"It is very simple. Time is of the essence. In ten days, Roger and I were to present at the Continental Geological Society's annual conference. I shall make the presentation alone. In order to do that, I must take him back to Lyme Regis, see him buried in the churchyard with Papa, and then proceed via the packet from Hampstead Heath back to Paris, where our hotel is already booked." She frowned at her sausages. "I wonder if they will charge me for both rooms." She shook her head. "Rooms will be in great demand. I doubt they will have any difficulty if I cancel one."

Georgia had lost the power of speech somewhere along this orderly train of events.

"But … I believe arrangements are being made to inter

your brother here, Miss Campbell," Millie said. "In the family catacomb. After a funeral mass."

Sibyl shook her head with finality. "Mama is a Methodist. She would be appalled at such a thing, to say nothing of not being able to visit his grave each Sunday. Even if she did somehow consent to his being buried here, she would not go down into the catacombs. No, I was up early this morning. I sent a tube to the train station, where the station master assured me a coffin could be procured and sent to the chateau this morning. He also reserved a seat for me in the first-class carriage at four o'clock this afternoon." She made a moue with her lips. "Second class does not permit cargo. Only luggage."

Georgia had never given any consideration as to whether a train ticket permitted cargo or not. Then again, she had never had to transport a coffin from one country to another.

"You are leaving today?" Millie asked. Her eggs, as yet untouched, were cooling on her plate. "This afternoon?"

"Yes, I just said so."

"But—but we—" Georgia laid a hand on Millie's arm, and the latter stopped.

"The doctor has expressed some doubt about Roger's death being … entirely natural," Georgia said. "It is his belief that he died from the same cause as his cousin Gregory."

"One does not need to be a doctor to observe that," Sibyl said briskly. "I suspected a heart attack, and this bears it out. No previous symptoms, otherwise healthy, then—" Her knife and fork sliced the last sausage neatly in half. "If you want my opinion, Lady Langford, there is a genetic defect somewhere in our lineage. Our father, you know, died suddenly as well."

"Of a heart attack?"

"In his case it was a fall while climbing in the Apennines,

but his loss of balance could have been preceded by a heart attack. He, too, was a healthy man in his prime." She laid her knife and fork at an equal distance from each other across her empty plate. "I will bid you farewell now, since I will be very much occupied in packing our things until I depart for the train. When she returns, please give the Countess de Valmy our most grateful thanks for her hospitality over the past weeks." She paused. "Do you think anyone would mind if I packed a few specimens in with Roger? It would save the cost of a third crate."

"I can't think why anyone would," Georgia said faintly. Except possibly the men lifting the coffin onto the train.

"I am sure Roger himself would approve," Millie managed. "Sibyl, are you certain you are up to this? Last night—forgive me, but last night you were in shock and nearly unable to function."

"But I woke this morning feeling a kind of relief at the monumental task ahead of me. Taking him home is the last thing I may do for my brother. I find the prospect comforting." With a final inclination of the head, she rose and left the room.

Millie stared at the door, as though she half expected her to come back in tears after such a brave performance, but she did not. Then Millie picked up her fork and began to eat rather as an automaton might, one bite after the next with no apparent enjoyment.

Georgia picked up her fork. After a moment, she said, "Millie, do you think we ought to offer to convey the Campbells to Lyme in *Helena*? We could be there and back by dinnertime."

Millie took a fortifying sip of the *café au lait* of which they had both become rather fond. "I do not. You heard her. She finds the making of arrangements and the overcoming of difficulties comforting."

"One would say that, wouldn't one, if one had no other option?"

"I do not think Sibyl is that kind of person. In any case, if we did do so, she might ask what you meant by the circumstances being not entirely natural. That must not get out, Georgia, or we shall have to contend not with one scandal, but with two."

Oh, dear. "It just slipped out," she confessed. "I will be more careful in future."

Millie nodded. "We both must watch our tongues. Are you going to call on the Villiers?"

"Yes, as soon as I may decently do so. Luckily, people keep country hours here, and I will not have to wait until after one o'clock."

"Then I will see the apothecary and Hortense, if you and Jean-Pierre will convey me to town first, and collect me afterward."

Georgia eyed her. "You see? We are doing the same as Sibyl. Making plans and arrangements to ward off the terror and the loss."

"But if we do not do it, who will?"

A very good question indeed.

9:50 a.m.

Millie watched Jean-Pierre and the steam landau bear Georgia away to the Villiers estate, and turned toward the apothecary's shop. She did not envy Georgia her errand; in

187

fact, she felt rather lucky to have the lighter side of the bargain.

A bell rang over the shop door as she pushed it open, and she breathed in the scent of rosemary and lavender, as well as the tang of … tea? She took in the shelves that rose to the ceiling, bearing wooden boxes of tea, jars of what looked like preserves with wax seals, corked beakers containing various liquids displayed in brass racks, and porcelain pots of creams and balms. Tiny bottles lay in an open box like a paintbox on the oak and glass case that did double duty as a counter, each bottle carefully labeled in a neat hand. *For anxiety. For depression. For minor wounds.*

A man in a canvas apron bustled out of the rear of the shop, four more tiny bottles in his hands. "Bonjour, madame. I will be with you in a moment. The doctor will be here shortly to collect his case. It must be refilled periodically."

"I am acquainted with Doctor Besson," Millie said. "This seems a very complete miniature apothecary. How clever of you both to have conceived it."

"Thank you, madame." He smiled, clearly pleased. "The doctor was very precise in his requirements. It saves time when minutes can mean the difference between a recovery and …" He trailed off, placed the last bottle in its niche, and closed the case with a double snap of its brass clasps. "Now, then. What may I do for you?"

"I have come for a bottle of the blueberry syrup you sent to Madame Laurent at the chateau yesterday," Millie said, doing her best to look harmless and pleasant. "It was delicious, and I should like some for my own gal—er, kitchen."

The apothecary tilted his head, mildly puzzled. "Madame Laurent?"

"I do beg your pardon. Jean-Pierre, the footman, would have been the actual person to have fetched the syrup. Madame, you see, was making individual desserts for the guests. Each one contained a separate compôte—raspberry, plum, blackberry. She was short one flavor, so she sent the footman, who chose the blueberry."

He was already shaking his head. "Jean-Pierre was here, madame, but I gave him no blueberry syrup. He was after powdered extract of *tribulus terrestris.*"

That did not sound promising. Or edible. "What is that, monsieur?"

"People call it puncture vine. The young men hereabouts have somehow come to believe it enhances the, er, well, the desire of women." He shook his head. "Every ten years or so there is a demand for it, they discover it doesn't do what their friends promise, and there is an end to it. I told Jean-Pierre I had none on hand, and that was that."

Millie did not want to think about young men dosing the girls of the village with extract of puncture vine. "So he did not take away blueberry syrup for the chateau?"

"*Non, madame.* If he had, I would have said so. I know the contents of every bottle in my shop."

"I never doubted it, monsieur," Millie said hastily. "Ah well, I shall have to do without. I had a lovely tea the other day, though—almost floral, and scented with lavender. I don't suppose you are the purveyor of it?"

"I am the creator of it, madame." With a flourish, he reached into the case and presented a small square tin painted with lavender flowers. When he opened the lid to reveal a muslin bag filled with tea leaves, the scent of the lavender tea she had enjoyed so much wafted out. Millie bought it on the spot, and left the shop on the best of terms with its proprietor.

During the walk down to the stonemason's house to give her tincture to Hortense, she turned over in her mind the discrepancy between Madame Laurent's blueberry syrup and Jean-Pierre's puncture vine. She would definitely confirm what the latter had gone to the apothecary for on their return trip to the chateau. And if he admitted to coming away empty-handed, then she and Georgia had a rather terrifying problem.

For why would madame lie to Georgia about the syrup?

There could be only one reason. She had made up the story out of whole cloth, thinking that it would never occur to a lady of quality to check her facts. And such an innocuous story, too. Easily believable. Merely the doings of the servants.

There had definitely been blueberry syrup in that Baked Alaska. The rancid scent of it had clung to Roger Campbell's sheets and pillow. Millie's had contained raspberry sauce, and Georgia's plum. If memory served, Monsieur Martin had enjoyed apple preserve, and Sibyl quince. None of them had suffered so much as a twinge. The blueberry had definitely been meant for Roger, despite what Madame Laurent had told Georgia about their being no order to the service of the desserts, or catering to personal preference, either.

But for goodness sake, why? Granted, Roger had been a bit of a self-centered boor, and careless of his sister's career, to say nothing of her feelings. But how could that be enough for a woman of Madame Laurent's standing to want to poison him?

And what about his cousin Gregory, who to Millie's knowledge, had no such defects of personality, but was a brilliant engineer, a loving husband, and a careful father. What could madame possibly have against him serious enough to do him fatal harm?

Millie had no answers, only more questions. But she had arrived at the neat stone wall of the Rivard home, so was forced to set them aside until she could talk them over with Georgia. The little maid let her in and led her back to Hortense's room, where she found her with Dr Besson. She handed Lali the jar in her reticule, and the girl hastened out to make the tea.

"Madame Brunel." The doctor's smile was sincere, if very weary. He could not have had more than a few hours' sleep the previous night, yet here he was, caring for his patient as if his entire day was at her service.

"I am glad to see you, doctor," she said. "I was just in the apothecary's shop. He has your case ready."

He nodded. "I will go along, then. Hortense, is there nothing more I may do for you? Can I bring you a favorite tea or syrup from the apothecary?"

"No, doctor. Thank you." She could not quite conjure a smile, but Millie was certain that the grey cast to her skin had lightened since she was last here.

Dr Besson bowed to Millie and departed, so she seated herself on the wicker chair and took the young woman's hand. "How are you feeling, dear?"

"I … do not know. I could not answer the doctor when he asked me, either."

"Your speech comes a little easier."

"I find my thoughts are not as confused. I felt yesterday as though I were in a dream."

"That is something. Dr Besson changed your dressing? Did he see improvement?"

"I was not any worse."

Millie could not help a surge of compassion. "Then we will call it improvement. For if one is not walking down into the valley of the shadow of death, my dear, one is climbing out of it. That is my philosophy, anyway."

A smile flickered on her lips, and this time Millie was certain it was not a spasm of pain.

While they waited, she resorted to the comfort of small, homely things. "I have been to the apothecary, as I said to the doctor. I was in search of some blueberry syrup to put in our little galley aboard *Helena*, my niece's and my airship, but the dear man had none. He did, however, have a lovely lavender tea on hand, so I did not leave empty-handed."

"You must ask *grandmère* for it, madame," Hortense whispered. "Hers is the best I have ever tasted. My husband says that if you have not had it drizzled on fresh sliced peaches, you have not lived."

Millie felt herself come to attention like a hunting dog scenting its prey. "I should like very much to try it. But alas, it is not yet the season for blueberries."

"She always has it on hand. It was a particular favorite of *le vicomte*, rest his soul. *Grandmère* told me that when he and his cousin visited as younger men, they would tease my mother that her only dowry need be the recipe for the blueberry syrup."

Here was news. "Your mother knew them as younger men?"

"*Oui*, she worked at the chateau. The upstairs maid. My grandparents lived in Montpelier then, in the employ of the

Duc de Sancerre. It was only after I was born that they came here."

"I see." A pattern was taking shape in Millie's mind. A pattern with dropped stitches—holes where a young man's infatuation with a woman his family would never approve might fit.

Hortense sighed. "I beg your pardon, madame, but I am very tired."

"I reproach myself for allowing you to talk so long," Millie said, patting the hand she held and laying it gently on the coverlet. "You will wake in an hour to drink the noon dose of tea?"

"If I do not, Lali will see to it. She is a harder taskmaster than the doctor." Her eyes were already closing.

Millie slipped out to find Lali hovering close by. "Is she better, madame?" she whispered anxiously.

"I will not say it in front of Doctor Besson, but I feel that she is," Millie whispered back. "If she recovers, it will be entirely due to the care of *le bon Dieu* … and you, Lali."

The girl was so overcome at the compliment that she began to cry, dabbing at her cheeks with her apron. Millie patted her shoulder, then let herself out and walked rapidly down the lane into the town. From across the square, she spied the Valmy landau waiting in front of the church, Georgia looking pensive, Jean-Pierre in the pilot's seat gazing at all and sundry like a lord surveying his acres.

Millie increased her pace. She had one question for him, and the sooner she had the answer, the better.

CHAPTER FIFTEEN

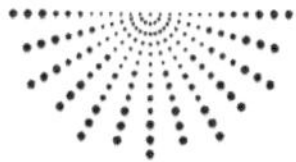

2:45 P.M.

Sibyl did not appear for lunch with Georgia and Millie. She did, however, say a courteous farewell to them before she climbed into the estate vehicle in which Anne had greeted them that first day. A coffin, nailed closed, and a square wooden crate kept company with her traveling trunk in the rear compartment. The driver pulled a cord, produced a whistle, and the conveyance chugged off without further ado.

"And so we are the last," Millie said as the sound faded.

Georgia hoped she did not mean it literally. They set off up the gravel avenue toward *Helena*. "I've been wanting to ask for hours, Millie. What was that you were asking Jean-Pierre about on the way in from town? I was in the rear and could not hear properly."

"I wished to know if he had bought a powder of puncture vine."

Georgia did not want to know why. It sounded appalling. "I thought he went to fetch blueberry syrup."

"The apothecary was most emphatic. Jean-Pierre wanted

195

puncture vine. Apparently it increases the ardour of young ladies, though it does not strike me that he needs any help in that department."

Georgia's worst fears were realized. "So Madame Laurent lied to me."

"It is worse than that—apparently she always keeps blueberry syrup on hand. Georgia, she is *renowned* for it. When Gregory and Roger visited as young men, they amused themselves by telling her daughter Genevieve she needed no other dowry but the recipe for that syrup."

"But … the Laurents were not yet in residence then."

"Genevieve worked here as the upstairs maid." Millie said no more until they were safely in the saloon. "Add that to Gregory's eye color and—"

Georgia sat rather suddenly on the sofa. "And Genevieve becomes the woman Gregory could not marry. Does Hortense know she is his daughter?"

"I do not think so. No father came into the conversation. According to the Laurent plaque in the chapel here, Genevieve died in childbirth, still unmarried."

She must breathe. And consider how these facts changed the picture they were attempting to construct. After several minutes, she shook her head. "I am at a loss to see how the events of seventeen years ago connect to the awful events of the last few weeks."

"I cannot see a connection, either," Millie admitted. "All I know is that some time after Genevieve died, the Laurents moved to the chateau to take up the positions they now hold. Hortense may have been sent to school, or been brought up right here on the estate. And no one said a word."

"Perhaps she met Monsieur Rivard when Gregory was

making improvements to the property after he inherited it." Georgia inhaled as a new and dreadful question presented itself. "If Hortense is his daughter, did Gregory know? And more, does Anne?"

"Would she have confided in you?"

Georgia had to conclude that she would not, and shook her head. But the mention of *Anne* and *confiding* had sparked something in her memory. But what? There were so many facts and speculations at war in her brain that she could not coax it out into the open.

Millie studied her face. "Let us leave this for now. Tell me what, if anything, you learned at the Villiers residence. Did you skewer the noble but untrustworthy Stefan and force him to a confession?"

Georgia made a sound in her throat that was the closest a lady might come to a snort of derision. "He was not at home. Apparently he and Madame Villiers' brother have been in Marseilles for three days, arranging for the latter to take up a position on a steamship bound for the Fifteen Colonies."

"Had enough of him, have they?"

"Madame is disappointed that her brother will be gone for at least a year, but she is bearing up. She confided to me that she hopes he will find a woman of good family to act as a steadying influence on him."

"So unless Stefan had some third party working for him—"

"Unlikely, surely."

"—he is not responsible for Roger's death."

"I do not think he is responsible for Gregory's, either," Georgia admitted. "According to Madame Villiers, their quarrels were always made up over port and cigars, and in truth, they deeply respected one another. She confided that Stefan has become a different man in the years since the engineering project began. He has a sense of purpose, she says, and is no longer the bored gentleman possessed of a superior education and no way in which to use it."

"I am glad," Millie said. "I hope his wife did not conclude that we suspected her husband of murder."

"No indeed. I couched all my remarks in the light of Roger's death, with sympathy as the unfortunate *vicomtesse's* oldest friend, and with respect as the representative of the family carrying the sad news."

"You realize what this means," Millie said slowly, after a moment.

"Oh, yes. The doors are closing one by one, leaving so few open that I feel we must make a choice between them. But I still cannot connect the highly respected Madame Laurent with two murders. My instinct tells me that she killed them both, but my reason demands to know why, and privately thinks my instinct is mad as a hatter."

And still she prodded her memory, like a person who cannot stop exploring with her tongue the space where a tooth has been.

"It must have something to do with her daughter," Millie mused. "But I cannot see how, especially in Roger's case. Bringing up old sorrows will be nothing but salt in the wound, and she is already offended that—"

"Salt!" Georgia said suddenly.

Millie stared at her, clearly believing her reason to be utterly in the right about her instinct.

"Salt," she repeated more calmly. "Valerie Boyle told me that after Anne had spoken with her husband, she quarrelled with Madame Laurent."

"You said the young lady would not break her mistress's confidence. Your conversation with her was closed."

"I've just remembered what she did say. Or what Anne said to her. *Too much knowledge lends as unpleasant a flavor to food as too much salt.* Anne was not eating, you see."

"And?"

"Too much knowledge, Millie. Think—Hortense is not yet seventeen. Gregory was known to have visited the Chateau de Valmy on more than one occasion as a young man, and later as well. What if—" She hardly dared say it. "What if, after his marriage to Anne, he met Genevieve again? What if, seventeen years ago, he made a grave error in judgment that resulted in Hortense's birth? What if *that* was the sin that he confessed to Anne that night? That made them quarrel?"

"And what if she sent for Madame to find out if it was true?" Millie covered her lips with her fingers. After a moment, she shook her head. "But even if it is ... Georgia, why now? Why not poison him then, when Madame found out he had so little respect for her daughter—to say nothing of his wife—that he could do such a thing?"

Georgia let out a long breath, feeling so frustrated she could scream. "I do not know. Why wait years to avenge your daughter's death? Why watch him have a family of his own and do nothing? Why now? What changed now? And what has poor Roger to do with any of this terrible history?"

Millie shook her head, clearly as unable to imagine any answers as Georgia. "He was here once as a young man, but that is the only visit we know of. He knew Genevieve, but he didn't love her as Gregory once did. What was *his* crime, that he should pay for it so dearly?"

"We cannot very well ask her."

"We may have to."

Georgia's mouth trembled. "But I want to see Mr Seacombe again, and I cannot do that if Madame poisons me."

"Do not think it, dearest. Despite Anne's instructions to the contrary, I really believe we should send for the gendarmes."

"And let *them* question Madame Laurent? She will lie to them as calmly as she lied to me this morning. I must say, Millie, she is the most skilled liar I have ever met. Even Hartford pales beside her." She swallowed, pushing the last vestiges of bitterness back down deep. "I find it difficult to reconcile a woman who may have killed two people with the grandmother who brought up an illegitimate child, protected her from the gossip of the neighborhood, and stood by her until she was safely the wife of a good man."

"People can have as many hidden chambers as my ammonite."

Which was true enough. "If not the gendarmes, then perhaps we ought to send for Anne."

Millie was already shaking her head. "If what we suspect is true, that woman has already killed half the family. Even if Anne could defend herself, would you bring those little girls into such danger?"

"No, indeed. I only mean it would be comforting not to be alone."

"You just mentioned someone who would come instantly to offer that comfort. Within hours, in fact."

"Oh, Millie," she sighed. "The temptation to hand the whole mess over to him and Mr van Meere is like a siren's call. But they cannot very well draw their six-guns and shoot her."

"They could, you know."

"We cannot put them in such a position. Somehow, we must convince Madame to confess her sins for the good of her soul, and allow herself to be delivered into the hands of the gendarmes."

"Georgia, that will never happen, and you know it."

"Then what are we to do?" One elbow on the back of the sofa, she rubbed her forehead. Perhaps it would massage a solution out of her brain. "I cannot think of one course of action that does not involve confronting her and her cleaver."

A flash of movement next to her elbow made her jump and stifle a scream.

In the next instant, a bedraggled hen settled on to the sinuous carving that ran along the back of the sofa. A moment later, the other hen flew up, both of them now regarding her and Millie with curiosity.

"Goodness," Millie said to the nearest one. "Have you decided that we mean you no harm after all?"

The hen did not reply, simply turned her head and preened what few feathers she possessed.

"I am happy that you feel safe now," Millie said softly to the bird. "I just wish that we could say the same."

4:05 p.m.

There was nothing for it. With only one door of possibility left open, Georgia bearded the lion in the morning room.

Madame Laurent glanced at Millie, who stood to the rear of the escritoire where Georgia was seated. Millie had removed the fireplace poker from its wrought-iron rack, and concealed it in the tall Canton vase of blue and white porcelain next to her, where she could snatch it up in a moment if necessary.

"I am sorry to interrupt your work for the second time today, Madame Laurent," Georgia began, laying down the pen with which she had been attempting to organize her thoughts.

"Is there a change to the dinner menu, madame?" The woman's calm would have been soothing had not Georgia suspected it to be rooted in a vast unconcern for the feelings, the hopes, the very lives of anyone outside her own family. This, at least, was the only way Georgia had been able to fathom her.

"With the departure of Miss Campbell—" *And her brother.* "—we are still dining *a deux*. No, madame, the nature of this interview is much more serious than that. Do sit down."

She seated herself in the chair she had used that morning, and waited.

Georgia breathed in. Out. Then began. "It appears you have told me an untruth. You did not send Jean-Pierre for blueberry syrup yesterday, because you always keep a supply on hand. In fact, I understand that it is a favorite among guests and family alike."

A pleat appeared between the greying brows. "Did I not? I was certain I did."

"The apothecary informed Madame Brunel this morning that Jean-Pierre's errand was to request powder of puncture vine," Georgia went on. "He was very specific."

"Perhaps the blueberry was on another occasion. I apologize, madame. I did not mean to mislead you."

Georgia did not believe that for a minute. "You told me a second untruth. You said that the Baked Alaska desserts were interchangeable. That the blueberry could have gone to anyone."

A small smile that almost held affection curved the woman's mouth. "It is true that *le vicomte* was particularly fond of my blueberry syrup. Yes, madame, I did imply they were interchangeable. But I served Monsieur Campbell the blueberry because he, too, was fond of it. At Chateau de Valmy, we pride ourselves on remembering the little preferences of our guests, in order to make their stay here as pleasant as possible."

"It is interesting that you should say so. We have also learned that both *le vicomte* and Roger Campbell stayed here as young men, and later, that Gregory Campbell visited the old vicomte following his own marriage."

"That is true," the cook said. "At least, the second part. I cannot attest to the earlier visits, as my husband and I were in the Duc de Sancerre's service at that time."

"It seems that both men were acquainted with your excellent syrup," Georgia said. "It became a favorite."

Madame waited, her chin tilted just a little, as if acknowledging a compliment.

"That is why, I suppose, you used it to conceal the flavor of the juice of monkshood root with which you poisoned both of them."

If a cannonbomb had detonated in the elegant morning room, the cook could not have looked more shocked. Her mouth fell open, then closed. Opened again as though to speak, but no words emerged. The color drained from her face and she clutched the seat of her chair with both hands, as though afraid she might fall off.

It only took an accusation of murder, Georgia thought fleetingly, to rock the woman's imperturbable calm.

"How—how—"

"How did I know?"

"How dare you?" Madame's eyes narrowed to slits, the words choked out in a whisper.

Beside the Canton vase, Millie stirred.

"I dare because my friend *la vicomtesse* is not here to ask you these questions," Georgia said, wishing she had a better weapon at hand than a pen. "I dare because her husband was an honorable man who did not deserve—"

"Honorable!" Madame barked the word. "Do you call it honorable for a man to betray his marriage vows? To take to his bed a young woman who had no choice in the matter, thus ruining her chances of marriage with a good man?"

Was this what happened? Georgia wondered. Had it been against her will, or had a love long denied overcome prudence? Not that it made a difference. Gregory was still at fault. Had still betrayed his wife. And his position of trust as Genevieve's employer.

"Did Genevieve ever tell him Hortense was his?" Millie asked.

"No. My daughter had too much pride, and returned to us in Montpelier before the child's birth. How do you know her name?" The words were flung at Millie like so many bits of gravel.

"The plaque in the church," she said simply.

"How did you manage *le vicomte*'s death?" Georgia asked. Poor Roger's was clear enough, but she had never been able to discover how Gregory had ingested the poison.

"La vicomtesse is accustomed to taking tea with her

husband each afternoon, in the English manner," madame said stiffly. "Several drops in the bottom of the cup are quickly concealed by the milk's being poured first. *La vicomtesse* needed explicit instructions as to the order."

Millie gasped.

Georgia must have misheard. "I beg your pardon?"

"Madame," the cook said quietly, "please do not force my confidence."

"I can and I will," Georgia snapped. "Explain what you just said to us or I will have you sacked without a character, and spread calumny as thick as lemon curd upon your name through every province in France." She felt sick, her hands and feet cold.

It could not be true. Anne could not have conspired with this woman to murder her husband. Impossible. She *loved* him.

Madame blinked at her tone, and drew a shaky breath. "No one was to know."

"We know. Doctor Besson knows. And Anne knows we know. I wrote several days ago to inform her."

"But you have not received a reply."

Georgia was silenced. She herself had sent Anne and the girls to the highlands of Scotland. Where the arm of French law, no matter how long, could not reach her. Of course Anne would not reply. Confess her sins in writing? Not likely.

Madame took a deep, shaky breath. "My daughter and Gregory Campbell had an *affaire de coeur* when he was a young man, visiting his relatives at the chateau. When he returned to university in Scotland, I could tell even at a distance that her heart went with him. Her letters to us at Montpelier were full of him—full of her hopes that they might marry. It was heartbreaking, madame, to read them knowing that the family would never permit it. One of the possible heirs and the upstairs maid? No, certainly not."

"So he married Anne."

"And still Genevieve loved him. Kept her position here at de Valmy in hopes of seeing him, even though he was no longer available to her. Then, a few years after his marriage, he came. And …" She made a motion with her hand that indicated the progression of events. "She returned to us when she began to show. The birth was terrible. Even now I cannot bear the memory. She died that same morning, leaving a beautiful girl."

"With his eyes," Millie said softly.

"When the opportunity came to take up a place here, I took it, not because I wished to look into those eyes in *his* face day after day, but because Hortense deserved to know her roots. We never told her who her father was, but she is an intelligent child. All she had to do was look in a mirror." After a moment of sad silence, she said, "All *la vicomtesse* had to do was look at *her*. Until she could no longer bear it."

"But why now?" Millie sounded as though she could not keep the words back.

Madame Laurent looked up. "Because of the baby."

"Hortense's baby?" Millie asked. "Jean-Joseph?"

"*La vicomtesse* had the news that it was a boy. He was illegitimate, but a boy in the direct bloodline may apply to the Court of Inheritance for some share of the estate. *Le vicomte* told her he was going to allow it. They quarreled. Then she came to me."

"And the little boy died," Millie whispered. "But not until after Gregory had consumed that cup of tea."

Madame bowed her head.

Georgia gathered her wits with difficulty. She must not think of Anne just now. That must come later, when she could weep for the loss of her oldest friend, who had somehow concealed her real self and built a mirage of a loving friend, a devoted wife, and a capable mother for all the years they had known each other.

"Why Roger?" she managed. "What had he done?"

"Assumed the mantle of *le vicomte*'s heir. You saw how he behaved. His disregard of the staff. His anger at you, madame, for usurping his place."

"Anne herself put me in charge," Georgia protested.

"And wisely so. *La vicomtesse* is certain she is carrying a boy. The kinship ties of all the other possible heirs are far enough removed that if it is a girl, it will be years before a decision is made as to the new vicomte, and she may continue to reside here. But Roger, he is first cousin. Even if she bears a boy, Roger too could apply to the court. He would not win, but her son would not be able to inherit for months, possibly years. She told me to act, and so I did."

Georgia thought rather dazedly that Hortense should be thanking her lucky stars Anne had not ordered her grandmother to slip a few drops of monkshood into *her* tea.

"What will you do now, madame?" Madame Laurent asked gently. "You will not turn me in to the gendarmes, will you, for obeying the directives of my mistress? For I have served her long enough to be aware that I, too, had no choice. She would have maligned me throughout France every bit as thoroughly as you, and my husband and I cast out to take refuge with any relative who would have us."

"I cannot very well do that, can I?" Georgia sighed. "You

were not in the room. She handed that cup of tea to Gregory herself, knowing full well what was in it. And while we have proved that the dessert Roger consumed contained the poison, no one in the kitchen would be able to stand before a tribunal and state unequivocally that you—and by extension, your mistress—meant that particular dessert for him."

"And his body is now out of the gendarmes' reach," Millie put in. "No autopsy is possible, for it is unlikely the English authorities will send him back."

And so two respectable men—albeit with sins aplenty to atone for—were dead with no way to seek justice. This woman would get away with aiding and abetting. And Anne McLeod Campbell, Vicomtesse de Valmy, would sail through the rest of her life with no one the wiser, and no one to bring her to account.

Georgia's stomach heaved. Behind her eyes, a headache threatened.

She gazed at the sheet of crested stationery where she had been trying to write down the chain of events. DUCAT QUI PACEM CUPIT. *He who desireth peace leadeth.* Oh, how she had misinterpreted everything! For there would be no peace in the chateau with the head of the household a murderess.

CHAPTER SIXTEEN

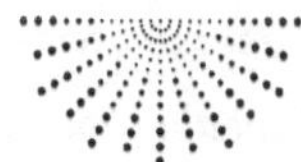

WEDNESDAY, JUNE 5, AT 10:16 P.M.

Georgia was just falling into an uneasy sleep in her cabin when the *clunk* of a pigeon arriving in the communications cage roused her as effectively as a trumpet next to her ear.

A letter from Mr Seacombe! Perhaps his and Mr van Meere's patience had worn through, and even now *Foresight* was sailing south. Wrapping her dressing gown about her, she hurried astern and found the pigeon cooling on the teak decking.

Helena's pigeon. She had only sent the one.

She removed the letter, shelved the pigeon on its rack, and hurried back to her cabin.

Millie hovered in the doorway, a moonglobe in her hand. "Is it—?"

"Not from *Foresight*, no. Ours." Millie peered at the elegant loops of Anne de Valmy's hand.

They hurried into the salon, she lit a lamp, and the two of them sat close together to read.

Dearest Georgia,

Forgive my silence when you deserved an instant reply to your inquiries. Especially when you, Miss Brunel, and Dr Besson have been so clever as to divine the cause of Gregory's death. There is some relief in knowing facts. But I am afraid all I am capable of in this letter is guesswork and supposition.

It has taken me several days to decide how much to tell you, and what, for Gregory's sake, I should conceal. But since I left you there without recourse or protection, I have concluded it is my duty to answer you truthfully. You said you needed only motive and opportunity. I will do my best to provide both, and may God forgive me.

The nature of my quarrel with Gregory that day is as old as Cain and Abel, I suppose. A child was born to Monsieur and Madame Rivard in the village—a little boy who did not survive. This boy was Gregory's unacknowledged grandson. His mother, Hortense, is Gregory's eldest daughter, which I have known for some years.

"She *knew?*" Millie exclaimed.

In the early years of our marriage, Gregory visited his elderly relation at the chateau, and met a woman called Genevieve, the only surviving child of the Laurents, with whom he had been in love as a young man. It seems that despite his marriage to me, they still harbored feelings for one another, and Hortense was the result. This, you may imagine, nearly destroyed me. It was the most difficult period of my life. I picked up the pieces of my dreams of what could be, put them away, and plodded on with what I had.

However, over the next eight years or so, something changed inside my husband. Some decision was made which caused him to renew the marriage vows in his heart that he had only made in his head before. And yes, while my trust had been broken, my love had persisted. Like the weeds in the garden, while the leaves could be pulled up, the root stubbornly lived on, unseen, under the soil. I was willing to join him in these vows. Elodie and Elise were the result of that commitment—a dual blessing for two people who had learned forgiveness as much as how to love again.

"Oh, Anne," Georgia whispered, her throat thickening with tears. To have reconciled and recommitted to each other, only to have their future so cruelly torn away!

The quarrel you heard of had to do with Hortense's little boy. Gregory wanted to inform the Court of Inheritance that he was willing for the child to have a portion of the estate upon his death. I, as you may imagine, was not. I even called in Mme L for moral support, thinking she would agree with me, since she had not allowed Gregory any contact with Hortense as a child. Even now I do not think the girl knows who her father is, though I suspect there is many a gossipy old biddy in the town who would be happy to tell her if they did not fear her grandmother so much. In any case, Madame did not agree with me, and so I ended the day in disgrace with both my husband and my cook, and took to my bed to sulk. As you know, dear friend, a tendency to sulk is one of my failings.

And then that poor little baby died, and Hortense was not expected to survive her ordeal. My heart broke for the Laurents—if you have been in the chapel since the funeral, you will have seen evidence of the sad fortunes of the family. That baby boy would have been the apple of their eye, the most beloved child in the whole town.

I tried to express my sympathy and hopes for Hortense's survival to Mme L, but she rebuffed them in no uncertain terms. I was taken aback by the simmering rage I saw in her eyes. Rage at fate, at poor Dr Besson's inability to save the baby or now the mother, at the fate of her family ... I still do not know for certain.

I only came to suspect that her rage had been directed entirely at Gregory later, after I received your letter, during these dreadful nights when I have not been able to sleep. I believe that in her eyes, he was responsible for what her family had come to—she and her husband alone in the world with no children or grandchildren to ease their old age. Had he not reunited with Genevieve, she might have married honorably and had a large family. But he did, and she died, and so did that little boy, their last hope. I do not know Hortense's condition. I hope it has improved.

Yes, this is all supposition, but I warned you. If Mme L is growing monkshood in the kitchen garden, then you and Millie and the doctor and I are the only ones who know it. Be very, very careful, dearest. If my suppositions provide motive, then perhaps something that kept me awake last night may provide opportunity.

Since receiving your letter, I have thought of nothing but the events of that awful day that was supposed to be such a happy celebration. And then the most everyday of private customs, so taken for granted I did not even remember it, struck me yesterday.

At university, Gregory and I got into the habit of taking tea together before our evening classes. That habit continued into our marriage, and became a daily ritual as we caught up on each other's bits of news before it was time to dress for dinner. The habit was broken during the dark years, but after the twins' birth it became a welcome respite from nappies and noise. That afternoon of the day he died, we took tea as usual. He did not complain of any bitter flavor, though I believe the tea was a new one—we did like to experiment. If I remember correctly, it was some smoked jasmine blend from India.

I have no proof of any of the following, so do with it what you will. But Gregory took his tea with lemon, and I with milk. That day, I remarked how considerate Mme L was in already squeezing the lemon for him, and pouring into my cup just the right amount of milk. That was at five o'clock. By midnight, he was dead. If this is truly how she did it, and the juice of monkshood was in his cup, my blood runs cold.

I send this to you for good or ill, and say again, be careful, dearest.

With all my love,

Anne

Georgia's hand shook so that the paper rattled and she was forced to hand it over to Millie.

After reading the final paragraphs, Millie laid it on the low table before the sofa. "I am … I do not … I …"

Georgia knew exactly what she meant. "Nor I."

"How can this be?" Millie asked, but whether of herself or Heaven above, Georgia did not know. "One lady is innocent, the other the most clever liar I have ever met. But which is which?"

Georgia collected her thoughts, which had been crashing about in her brain like a flock of frightened pigeons. "Anne insists that what she says is supposition. But Millie, let us consider for a moment. Anne had no reason I can fathom to do away with her husband. They had reconciled, they were happy, they both had a place in the world they valued and children they loved. Even if she still harbored a little resentment deep in her heart at his betrayal, it could never have been enough to compel her to kill him."

"Whereas Madame Laurent harbors not only a furious

resentment bordering on hatred, if Anne's assessment is accurate, she also presides over a poison garden. Which Anne is forbidden to enter."

"Monkshood in the *teacup*," Georgia said on a long breath. "Though she said it was in the milk. Not the lemon. Another lie."

"Either way, the very thing we could not fix upon," Millie agreed. "*How* and *when* the poison was administered. And of course, by the time Gregory's symptoms became acute, the evidence had long been cleared away, the dishes washed, and the house abuzz with celebrating guests."

The face of Madame Laurent rose up in Georgia's memory like a spectre. "No wonder she looked as she did when I accused her point blank this afternoon of killing both men. How clever she is, to recover so quickly. To immediately turn both sets of facts around so that they pointed to Anne as the poisoner by proxy!"

"Your previous interview with her must have made her realize how precarious her position is," Millie said slowly. "She has likely been awake at night since then, carefully adjusting the facts to be most convincing. Even to include Anne's delay in replying to point to her guilt."

"That was what I believed to be the nail in Anne's metaphorical coffin, I am ashamed to say," Georgia said sadly. "I shall have to beg her forgiveness if I ever see her again. All these years of friendship, and I abandoned my faith in her so quickly. I am a fool, Millie."

Millie laid a comforting hand on hers and squeezed it. "There is no shame or foolishness in the case, to have been taken in by so accomplished a creature. I too was convinced she was only obeying her mistress's direction."

"Her reasons for doing away with Gregory are completely believable. I am not convinced, however, that a second man must be killed simply for lording it about the chateau. She must have seen that Roger was harmless. Annoying, but harmless."

"But we do have proof that his death is on her hands," Millie said. "In a very literal sense. Her assistants in the kitchen may not have seen her slip a few drops of juice into that dessert, but we all witnessed her carry it directly to Roger, and smelled it on the sheets after he was dead."

"That is true. I suppose the *what* and the *how* are more important to the gendarmes than the *why*, in his case." She glanced at her companion. "We must inform them, Millie. I shall write the letter here, and send a tube from the morning room." She gently laid Millie's hand aside and rose.

"What, now?"

"The longer we wait, the more likely we are to find something equally unpleasant in our own teacups. Yet if we take our meals aboard *Helena*, or go into Valmy saying we wish to enjoy a restaurant, she will suspect we do not trust her. We may be able to fudge oversleeping tomorrow, but after that, we have only half a day at most."

Département de la gendarmerie
Prefecture d'Arles
Provence

I am writing to inform you that the murderer of le Vicomte de Valmy has been discovered. The guilty party is Madame Laurent, the cook at the chateau, who poisoned both le vicomte and his cousin, Monsieur Roger Campbell, a guest in his home, with root of monkshood, which she grows in the kitchen garden.

Madame Laurent's reason for murdering le vicomte is her rage at his impregnating her daughter, Genevieve Laurent, who died nearly seventeen years ago during the birth of her illegitimate child. That child, Mme Hortense Rivard, lies at death's door after the birth of her own legitimate son. These losses, it seems, have affected the mind of Madame Laurent, who has taken revenge on the men of the de Valmy family in a most painful and agonizing way.

I beg that you will send gendarmes immediately to arrest her, as we, the remaining guests in the chateau, are now in grave danger should she learn that her crimes have been brought to light. Madame Laurent will tell you that she acted upon the instructions of Anne, Vicomtesse de Valmy, who has fled to Scotland to protect her children and is not in France to defend herself. However, I am in full possession of the facts, and implore that you do not delay your flight here to apprehend this woman. For corroboration of all I have said, you may apply to Dr Besson of the town of Valmy, who attended both deaths and has been of great assistance in helping us discover the truth.

I remain
Yours most faithfully,
Georgia Brunel, Lady Langford
Chateau de Valmy

Georgia did not dare go down to the chateau in only her dressing gown, so she dressed simply in skirt and blouse and chemise, dispensing even with a corset. Instead of her half-boots, she slipped on a pair of soft leather flats that resembled ballet shoes, which she tended to wear as slippers. They were both comfortable and quiet.

"I will be back in five minutes," she assured Millie.

"If you are not, I will come after you. That poker is still in the vase, and I am not afraid to use it."

Some might find such a promise frightening, but Georgia felt rather comforted as she hurried down the avenue on the grass between the gravel paths. Gravel was not kind to shoes such as these. The front door was locked, so she slipped around to the rear, to the door where all Anne's sun hats made pale circles on the wall. After that, it took but a minute to run up the stairs to the morning room.

By the light of a moonglobe, she chose a brass cylinder from the collection in the stand, and sealed the letter inside. She turned its dials to indicate the address in the town of Arles, and the pneumatic system sucked it away. With a sigh of relief, she closed the little door in the wall.

"What are you doing, madame?"

Georgia practically leaped out of her skin. She whirled to see Madame Laurent on the morning room's threshold, still fully dressed. She hoped the woman could not see her heart pounding as she lifted her chin.

"Until *la vicomtesse*'s return, I am châtelaine of this house. I may do as I see fit."

"Sending a tube at half past eleven at night? Normally a guest would summon Monsieur Chouinard, and he would look after it for you."

"I would not disturb him when I am perfectly capable of doing so myself." She strolled toward the Canton vase, still situated where Millie had left it, behind the escritoire. Not that she thought madame would assault her, but she felt safer with a piece of furniture between them.

Madame came farther into the room, to stand before the

cold hearth opposite. Now there was nothing between them but a short expanse of carpet.

"To whom are you writing, madame?"

If she said *none of your business*, she might make her angry. She must play the ally, not the antagonist. "If you must know, it was *la vicomtesse*. I feel betrayed, madame, that she has put the two of us in such a position. For I am responsible for the welfare of the people here in her absence. I am responsible for *you*, and regret to the core of my being that you have been forced to do what no person of morals should be asked to do."

"Thank you for that. I take it she has still not replied to your letter."

"No. I think we both know what that means. She will not admit to anything in writing. But I couched my letter just now in such terms that she may let something slip. Especially since I led her to believe that—" Oh, goodness. Who could she name? "—Père François is the object of my curiosity."

Madame frowned. "That is cruel. He would never hurt *le vicomte* or his cousin."

"I understand he had a vengeful temperament and a bad reputation as a younger man."

"But his vows to the church have thrown all that into the sea of forgetfulness."

"Not everyone shares your good opinion."

Somehow the woman had moved closer.

Regretting the necessity of abandoning the contents of the vase, Georgia slipped behind the escritoire and moved toward the door with every appearance of confidence. "Good night, madame. Sleep well."

"One moment, Lady Langford. I believe you will wish to see proof of what I said to you this afternoon."

Georgia paused on the threshold. "There is proof? May it not wait until morning?"

The cook shook her head. "We will both sleep better if we do not wait. Once you see it for yourself, in the morning you may wish to contact the gendarmes."

Georgia did not believe a word of it, but the less said about gendarmes, the better. "It must be incontrovertible." The woman nodded. "By all means, then."

The cook led the way along the corridor, then up the stairs to the family floor. For one dreadful moment, Georgia thought she meant to revisit the scene of one or other of her crimes.

Instead, she looked over her shoulder and waved at the open door of Anne's suite of rooms, where lamplight glowed dimly. "The lady's maid Valerie Boyle returned this evening. Her mother is much improved, apparently."

"I am glad to hear it. Mademoiselle Boyle was to take two weeks, and it has barely been one."

Along the corridor, she opened the door to the stairs up to the nursery and the staff bedrooms. "This way, madame."

"Have you concealed the proof in your room?" Georgia was perfectly willing to accompany her upstairs, where people were getting ready for bed or reading or being blessedly uncomplicated and human. Better than being lured into the woman's home, where goodness knew how many weapons hung in the kitchen.

"My husband and I occupy one of the senior staff cottages. No, I am afraid we must climb a little more."

And here was the narrow staircase that Manon Fleury had showed her. The cook hitched up her skirts in a businesslike way and began to climb the steep stairs. Georgia hesitated at the bottom. She didn't like the look of this at all. This proof very likely did not exist. Still, it was better to know what, if any, evidence madame could have twisted into being in order to implicate Anne.

"You have concealed it up here? I must say, it might have been easier to hide something in your cottage. Or in the forest."

"But then it might be accidentally found," the woman said over her shoulder. She was nearly at the top of the stair and not even out of breath.

Georgia made up her mind. If madame planned to denounce Anne publicly and then summon the gendarmes herself, she had better find out what she was up to. But she would be very much on her guard.

The other woman held open the door at the top, and Georgia emerged onto the roof. Immediately the wind snatched at her skirt and blew it flat against her legs.

"The weather is changing," madame observed. "I understand Madame Fleury showed you the rooftop one afternoon."

"Yes, she did." How on earth did she know that? But then, the servants came and went all over the house, and no doubt exchanged bits of what they saw and heard downstairs, no matter how trivial. "She said she used to come up here as a child, and even had a special place that overlooked the gardens where she would not be disturbed."

The moon came and went behind racing clouds, making Madame Laurent's figure seem to fade into the darkness and reveal itself from one moment to the next. "I was not here then, but she told me of it. Since she has now departed, I decided that this place would be the safest in which to conceal what I have to show you. You still have your moonglobe?"

Georgia patted her pocket.

Here was the narrow walk along the ridgeline of the slate roof. The ground was nearly invisible far below, coming and going in the moonlight much the way the woman ahead of her had done. Georgia's feet in the soft leather slippers felt the heat of the day still rising from the slates. Thank goodness for such a connection, since the wind was fierce.

Madame stood aside so that Georgia might precede her into the stone turret with the wide embrasures. At her appearance, pigeons exclaimed in alarm, but only one flew out over madame's head. The woman did not even flinch. Georgia shook her moonglobe into a glow and, just to be certain she had indeed been duped, cast around for a notebook or a heap of artifacts or anything resembling proof.

There was nothing there but pigeon droppings.

"Have you hidden it behind a stone, madame?"

"No, you fool. I am content to stand here and marvel at the haughty stupidity of the wealthy." Her tone dripped contempt.

"I am not such a fool as to believe a word of your story," Georgia replied, doing her best to keep her voice level though her heart was pounding. "For I did hear from Anne, who told me that you served her and *le vicomte* tea before the guests arrived for his birthday party. I suspect that the juice of monkshood was in the lemon you had so considerately squeezed into the cup beforehand."

Madame gazed at her, the angle of the moonglobe Georgia held creating black sockets in which her eyes glittered. The wind batted at her skirts in the archway, pulling at them, tearing at her neat ruffled cap and hair.

"Anne did not instruct you to kill her husband," Georgia went on. "You, madame, are alone guilty for allowing your hatred of him to force you to murder."

"I did not hate him enough to proceed beyond daydreams of his death … not until *ma pauvre petit* Jean-Joseph died," she said, the words clearly painful in her throat. "Hortense may not survive, and then Albert and I will be left alone in the world. It is that man's fault. He deserved what he got. De Valmy is the author and finisher of all my grief."

"And what part did Roger play that he should meet the same fate?"

Madame Laurent did not even bother to deny it. The time for pretense was past, and the words tumbled out of her as though sheer rage were propelling them.

"You were there at the table. You heard him speak of *ma chere* Genevieve in terms that no man should use of a respectable woman. *A summer fling. No better than she should be.* My beautiful daughter, to be spoken of by a landless fool such as he!"

He and Monsieur Martin had been speaking of their earlier visits to the chateau. Of the woman Gregory had been in love with. Georgia had to acknowledge that Roger's dismissal of Genevieve as just a housemaid, fair game for gentlemen, had indeed been offensive.

"Chouinard came downstairs and told me what indignities they were heaping upon her defenseless head and I—I—"

Dessert had taken a long time to arrive. "You introduced the monkshood to the blueberry syrup Genevieve had once told you he loved," Georgia said. "You knew he would not leave a drop."

"And he did not," madame said. "He did not even notice the

missing meringue where I inserted the spoon after it was baked."

Now was not the time to pontificate on the loose tongues of gentlemen following a good dinner with wine. Or their attitudes to women of any class but their own. "I thank you for confiding in me," she said, "and will forgive your incivility."

"Will you, now? Who were you sending that tube to?" She advanced into the stone chamber, where the wind was now whistling under the eaves with hollow sounds like the hooting of an owl. It did not bother the pigeons in the least. But they watched madame as warily as Georgia did.

She edged around the circumference of the chamber toward the door. Madame sidestepped and blocked the way.

"Who, madame? For it was not *la vicomtesse*, I'll wager."

"No, it was to the gendarmerie in Arles." Georgia dodged past her, only to have the woman whirl and grab her arm with a grip so fierce Georgia cried out. She dropped the moon-globe, which rolled out through the arch. A moment later came the rhythmic banging of the wretched thing as it bounced down the roof and disappeared into the darkness.

Madame bent Georgia's arm up behind her back and duck-walked her over to one of the embrasures. Georgia had felt this pain before at Hartford's hands. Excruciating pain that brought tears to her eyes. Her body reacted as it had then —foolhardy as it had been.

She stamped on madame's foot as hard as she could. The pain of a soft slipper landing on hard leather shoes arrowed into her brain, but the grip on her arm loosened just enough for her to twist away.

"You cannot run, silly woman," Madame Laurent panted.

Georgia made it to the archway and flung herself through it. It was only twenty yards to the door into the chateau—

Her skirt caught on something and she turned to release it. Her frantic hands landed on those of madame, who was already reeling her in by the fan of pleats in the rear.

Someone screamed and a ball of light flew at them out of the night. Georgia ducked and the moonglobe struck Madame Laurent on the ear. With a shriek, she released Georgia's skirt so suddenly that Georgia pitched forward to her knees at the same time as madame straightened and turned to confront this new threat.

But one foot met empty air.

Madame teetered, seeking purchase, but her own momentum made her tilt … her arms windmilled as she fought for balance—to regain the narrow walk. Georgia tried to catch her hand—missed—and with a scream that would echo in her nightmares for months, Madame Laurent fell on the steep slate roof. Her own weight could not stop her—her shoes, her hands scrabbled on the slates to no avail—not even the eaves with their watchful gargoyles could stop her from sliding over the edge … and plummeting into the blowing darkness.

CHAPTER SEVENTEEN

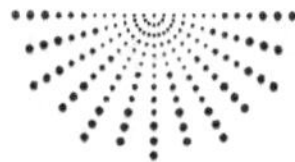

Georgia!" Millie shrieked. She flung down the poker with a clang of iron on stone, and ran headlong toward her on a ribbon of slate that seemed only wide enough to accommodate a cat. She must prevent her from taking the same fatal misstep—she could not bear it— Mr Seacombe would never forgive her—

"Madame Brunel!" Valerie Boyle chased her, clearly thinking she would have to haul them both up from the precipice.

The thought slowed her to a more circumspect but fast walk, all the while keeping her eyes fixed on the slates in front of her. She could not bear to look to the right, where —where—

She flung herself to her knees next to the person she cared about most in the world, who was crouched in a ball on the slates, the wind pulling at her blouse and hair. A pigeon perched below on a dormer, gazing at them as if they were all mad.

"Dearest girl, are you hurt? Tell me at once."

"Mesdames, we must get off this roof," Valerie said anxiously. "It will rain, and the slates even on this walk are dreadfully slippery."

"Yes," Georgia said faintly. "I mean, no, Millie, I am not hurt. And I would dearly love to get off this godforsaken roof."

"Come," Valerie said, helping Millie to her feet so that she could help Georgia to hers. "I will lead, and we will hold hands, as the children do."

Ten minutes of terror and a breathless descent of far too many stairs later, Valerie lit a lamp and guided them onto the sofa in the morning room. "Stay there," she said, and vanished.

They could not have moved another foot in any case. As thunder rumbled outside and the rain began, Georgia clung to Millie and burst into tears. They wept together—for their narrow escape, for another death, for the deaths that had preceded it. When Valerie returned with a tray bearing a decanter of brandy and three glasses, they were forced to mop their faces with the tray cloth and blow their noses on the young woman's handkerchief, having not so much as a petticoat ruffle between them.

Georgia knocked back a good gulp of brandy. Millie took hers more slowly, but still, it stole her breath and burned all the way down. Valerie sipped hers with all the respect such a fine vintage deserved.

When she recovered, Georgia gasped, "How? How did you both come to be up there?"

"I said I would follow you down if you were not back in five minutes." The second gulp went down Millie's throat a little easier. "I am a woman of my word. But you were not in the morning room, nor anywhere else on both floors. By the time I discovered Mademoiselle Boyle in my search, it was clear you were nowhere in the house."

"But I had heard Lady Langford speaking with Madame Laurent, and had looked out of the door of my mistress's room," Valerie said. "I saw them go up to the nursery. So we followed."

"I knew it could not be for any noble or rational reason that you were going up there," Millie said. "Valerie's room is on that floor, so she looked for you both. When you were nowhere to be found, our only option was the attic staircase."

"Thank dear heaven for your persistence." Georgia's cold hand closed around her own in gratitude. "The moonglobe—"

"We saw one fall off the roof. It helped us locate you. As for the other, that was Valerie."

"You will remember I have brothers," Valerie said, her face softening into a brief smile. "I have a good arm."

"Thank your brothers for me—I am alive at this moment because of that arm. The moonglobe hit her on the side of the head and she lost her balance. But I did not turn fast enough to catch her hands."

"She would have dragged you down with her," Millie said grimly. Simply to put an end to her enemy, even if it meant her own death. "Providence prevented it."

"Valerie—Millie—" Georgia began to cry once more, words of gratitude utterly beyond her. All she could do was grip their hands and sob.

When at length she recovered, Millie told Valerie what had happened following her departure the week before. Now it was the young woman's turn to take a less than respectful gulp of the brandy.

"*Mon Dieu*," she whispered. "The evil ... and in plain sight.

None of us suspected anything but a heart attack. The poor vicomte. And my mistress—how will she bear it?"

"She has her girls, and you, and Monsieur Martin to bear her up and help her," Millie said softly. "She appears to me to be a strong woman. Now that the true cause of her husband's death has been revealed and the gendarmes have been summoned, she will be able to return."

"But I will not be here." Valerie's eyes filled with tears. "Oh, mesdames, I cannot stay." She looked about her, as though Madame Laurent might yet step through the door. "So much death. I cannot endure it. I must go. Though where, I cannot tell."

"To your mother's, surely?" Georgia seemed all too happy to leave the subject of death behind and turn to more homely concerns. "I understand her health is improving?"

"Yes, because my brother and his family arrived to inform her that they will be moving into our family home. In one way it is a great relief to me, because she will be well looked after, but in another…" Valerie gave a one-shouldered shrug. "There is no room for me." She pasted on a brave smile. "I shall simply find another place. At least *la vicomtesse* will allow me to stay until I have another position, and will give me a good character, I hope."

Georgia sat up straight, as though someone had poured the brandy down the back of her neck. "Valerie … what if … tell me …" She took a deep breath and tried again. "Will the French authorities accept the commission of an English pilot? That is to say, if a person were to take their training in the English manner, would they be permitted to fly a French vessel?"

"Why, yes, madame. It would only mean a month's course

in aeronautical protocols specific to this country to be fully certified. It is the physical flight training as midshipman that takes two years."

"Then—then I invite you, my dear, to join our crew as midshipman. Millie and I are learning ourselves, but we have both aptitude and willingness to share with you. There is no reason why you may not do your training with us."

Millie's heart filled with admiration and gratitude for the generosity and the sheer aptness of such a brilliant solution.

Valerie, on the other hand, sat motionless, the brandy glass tilting slightly in her hand. Millie reached out and gently set it on the side table next to her elbow. "Do you like chickens, my dear?"

She blinked. Opened her mouth. Closed it again.

"I only ask because we have adopted a pair of hens. That bully of a butcher in Valmy was going to slaughter them because he said they don't lay." Righteous anger bubbled up inside again, but Millie pushed it down. "I must warn you that they are not to be eaten. They are our companions, come what may."

"I—I am very fond of chickens," Valerie managed. "Oh, mesdames, please tell me you are not amusing yourselves. Please do not toy with me in this way."

"When you come to know us better, you will realize that toying with people is foreign to both our natures," Georgia said firmly. "We are all in a state of horror and confusion at the moment—and someone must yet inform poor Monsieur Laurent that the misfortune of his family has been compounded tonight. But it is as clear to me as a summer day that if you want to fly, and your mother is to be cared for in the bosom of her family, then there is nothing left to keep your feet on the ground but your own wishes."

"I *do* want to fly," Valerie said in a whisper so fierce she may as well have screamed it. "I have always wanted it, from the days when all I could do was to climb a tree to be closer to the wind."

"Then fly with us," Millie said simply. "When Anne returns and all this is over, we three will become four."

"Three?"

"*Helena* herself is our third," Georgia said. "Named for my daughter, lost to me as a baby."

"I miscounted—we will be six," Millie corrected herself. "The hens."

Valerie laughed, and in her joy Millie had a glimpse of the dedicated, powerful woman she could become in fulfilling her dreams of chasing the wind. "Mesdames, I would be a fool to say no," she said, holding out her hands to both of them. They clasped hands on the bargain, then Georgia picked up her brandy to offer a toast.

"To flying close to the wind," she said.

The *ting* of three crystal glasses sounded for all the world like faraway bells, celebrating the blessings of friendship and love, no matter where the winds blowing into the future chose to take them.

EPILOGUE

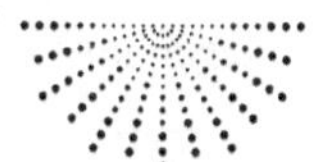

EXTRACT FROM A VERY LENGTHY LETTER
DATED JUNE 11, 1895

... and I can hear you now, remonstrating with me for being so foolish as to go up on that roof knowing what she was capable of. Be assured I had my reasons. The only foolish part was my belief that my comparative youth and mental preparation would save me. In the end it was Millie and Valerie who did so, one by distracting her with a scream and the other by throwing a moonglobe with astonishing accuracy.

So our crew has now increased by two hens and that brave young woman, who is determined to become a pilot. La vicomtesse is so shattered not only by her recent widowhood, but also by the realization that none of us—herself included—were willing to suspect a murderess simply because she was a woman of some renown. The fact that Millie and I are absconding with her lady's maid seems very minor in comparison. She handed over a glowing character reference with hardly a qualm. I do not think it has quite sunk in that Valerie will never dress hair again—though I have her promise she will teach me enough to do my own creditably, using the latest magazines from Paris.

I feel quite safe in leaving Anne to the tender care of Benezet

Martin, who confessed to me privately that he has been in love with her since their university days. Even if she never returns his love—which I doubt, given enough time—she will find a staunch supporter in him, one with enough knowledge to make the estate flourish. If the good Lord wills that she should have a boy in the autumn, then well and good. If He does not, then the next heir will find everything in perfect order thanks to Monsieur Martin ... once the Court of Inheritance in their wisdom determine who that might be.

I rather hope it is one of Manon Fleury's boys. Until the eldest is of age, she would make a wonderful châtelaine, and no one may tell her she cannot go anywhere on the estate. The poison garden is being dug up and the plants burned as we speak.

Poor Monsieur Laurent, it turns out, had no idea that his wife was the angel of doom presiding over the chateau. He is a broken man ... or would be, if his granddaughter had not begun to show clear signs of recovery. I am coming to think Millie might have a touch of magic about her. Dr Besson had given Hortense up, and yet under Millie's, her husband's, and her faithful little housemaid's care she improves a little every day. I stifled the urge to complain about the appearance of yet another enormous tome on the subject of herbal medicine, which appeared after church courtesy of the good doctor. Do not tell Mr van Meere she has made another conquest. It would be quite unkind, when we leave Valmy astern tomorrow.

Both Millie and I are anxious to see Langford Park again. After Teddy serves his summer internship with one of the Brunel connections in London (something to do with tunnels), he will join us. In September, then, I believe we three will be of the party at what Mr van Meere calls "this shindig in Cornwall." I quite look forward to meeting the Earl and Countess of Falmouth, to say nothing of Lady

Claire and Sir Andrew Malvern. Teddy has long held the latter in awe and has read everything either of them has ever published.

But most of all, I look forward to seeing our friends aboard Foresight. Should her great fuselage appear over the trees of Langford Park before September, we would be delighted. I do not think she will fit in the airfield, which is only designed for two smaller civilian ships. However, the Long Chase that extends for a mile to the north of the house will accommodate her very comfortably. I hope that her captain and crew will welcome young Valerie Boyle, and give both her and myself instruction in the intricacies of engine maintenance.

Please come. In the worst of the storm we have just weathered, the thought of you was my comfort and hope.

Your own

Georgia

THE END

AFTERWORD

Dear reader,

I hope you have enjoyed *The Engineer's Nemesis*, and our continuing adventures in the Magnificent Devices world via the Lady Georgia Brunel Mysteries. Georgia and Millie's adventures will continue in book four, *The Aeronaut's Heir*. Here is a sneak peek!

A child's empty bed compels Georgia and Millie to face an old enemy ... and their greatest fear

For the first time in her life, Georgia Brunel is surrounded by those who love her. Buoyed by happiness, she, Aunt Millie, and her son, Theodore, home from Oxford for the summer, take flight in the airship *Helena* for Cornwall. Along with their friends aboard *Foresight*, they are to attend the greatest scientific symposium of the decade. Hosted by the Earl and Countess of Falmouth, they will meet engineering luminaries from all over Europe and England—including Sir Andrew and Lady Claire Malvern.

The first day of the symposium goes off without a hitch.

But that night, the Falmouth heir, barely out of his infancy, is discovered missing from his bed. Even worse, Teddy Brunel is missing from his. Are the two disappearances connected? Was Teddy attempting to save the child? And what does a Venetian assassin's coin found under the bed mean—other than certain death for someone at the estate?

The house is full of the rich and famous. The reporters shouting at the gates must not get wind of this disaster. And the Prince Consort must be prevented from risking his life to come and award the prize for best invention. It is up to Georgia and Millie to swallow their fear for Teddy and the baby, and marshal their wits to help locate them. Along with a pair of Texican gentlemen with skills no gentleman should possess, they must work in the shadows to find the missing boys before time runs out … and takes the most precious person in Georgia's life with it.

> *"I found it refreshing to read something where the main characters are 'women of a certain age.' Both women have agency, intelligence, and the backbone to use them. Being women and products of their social class, they are limited in their ability to be taken seriously by those in charge, which makes the conflict organic. And look out for the chickens. There are always chickens." —Fanbase Press*

If this is your first visit to my cozy alt-history world, I hope you will begin your own adventures with the first books in my three connected steampunk series:

- *The Emperor's Aeronaut (The Regent's Devices 1, 1819)*

- *Lady of Devices* (Magnificent Devices 1, 1889)
- *The Bride Wore Constant White* (Mysterious Devices 1, 1895)

I invite you to visit my website to subscribe to my newsletter, browse my blog, and learn more about my books. Or visit moonshellbooks.com to buy directly from me.

Welcome to the flock!

Warmly,

Shelley

ALSO BY SHELLEY ADINA

STEAMPUNK

The Magnificent Devices series

Lady of Devices

Her Own Devices

Magnificent Devices

Brilliant Devices

A Lady of Resources

A Lady of Spirit

A Lady of Integrity

A Gentleman of Means

Devices Brightly Shining (Christmas novella)

Fields of Air

Fields of Iron

Fields of Gold

Carrick House (novella)

Selwyn Place (novella)

Holly Cottage (novella)

Gwynn Place (novella)

Acorn (novella)

Aster (novella)

Iris (novella)

Rosa (novella)

The Mysterious Devices series

The Bride Wore Constant White

The Dancer Wore Opera Rose

The Matchmaker Wore Mars Yellow

The Engineer Wore Venetian Red

The Judge Wore Lamp Black

The Professor Wore Prussian Blue

The Lady Georgia Brunel Mysteries

"The Air Affair" (prequel short story)

The Clockwork City

The Automaton Empress

The Engineer's Nemesis

The Aeronaut's Heir

The Texican Tinkerer

The Wounded Airship

The Regent's Devices series with R.E. Scott

The Emperor's Aeronaut

The Prince's Pilot

The Lady's Triumph

The Pilot's Promise (novella)

The Aeronaut's Heart (novella in anthology)

ABOUT THE AUTHOR

Shelley Adina is the author of some 60 novels published by Harlequin, Warner, Hachette, and Moonshell Books, Inc., her own independent press. She writes steampunk adventure and cozy fantasy historical mystery as Shelley Adina; as Charlotte Henry, writes classic Regency romance; and as Adina Senft, is the *USA Today* bestselling author of Amish women's fiction.

She holds a PhD in Creative Writing from Lancaster University in the UK; her dissertation was a historical women's fiction novel. She appeared in the 2016 documentary film *Love Between the Covers*, is a popular speaker and convention panelist, and has been a guest on many podcasts, including Worldshapers and Realm of Books.

When she's not writing, Shelley is usually quilting, sewing historical costumes, or enjoying the garden with her flock of rescued chickens.

Shelley loves to talk with readers about books, chickens, and costuming!

shelleyadina.com
moonshellbooks.com

www.ingramcontent.com/pod-product-compliance
Lightning Source LLC
Chambersburg PA
CBHW020755310726
48969CB00002B/548